"T...
Sa...
w...

Nora rubbed at the tightness in her throat with one ice-cold hand. "He wants to control Scotty." Her gaze speared Sabriel's jungle-green eyes. "I can't let that happen."

In the depth of his steady gaze, she found reassurance. For the first time in her life, someone was seeing her, and not flinching at what he saw there. He knew. He understood. The Colonel had almost broken him, too. But he'd survived, and that gave her hope. Heat returned to her cold limbs, and she wanted to linger there in the calming balm of his sight.

"We'll find your son."

She took his promise to heart.

"The Colonel wants his grandson," Gabriel said. "And what the Colonel wants, the Colonel goes after."

SYLVIE KURTZ

SPIRIT OF A HUNTER

TORONTO • NEW YORK • LONDON
AMSTERDAM • PARIS • SYDNEY • HAMBURG
STOCKHOLM • ATHENS • TOKYO • MILAN • MADRID
PRAGUE • WARSAW • BUDAPEST • AUCKLAND

In memory of Charlotte L. Bégin.
Her spirit of adventure will always be an inspiration.

A special thanks to Bill and Lorrie Thomson,
and Chuck Kurtz. For planning hikes in the
White Mountains, then making sure I survived. ☺

ISBN-13: 978-0-373-69271-2
ISBN-10:   0-373-69271-4

SPIRIT OF A HUNTER

ABOUT THE AUTHOR

Flying an eight-hour solo cross-country in a Piper Arrow with only the airplane's crackling radio and a large bag of M&M's for company, Sylvie Kurtz realized a pilot's life wasn't for her. The stories zooming in and out of her mind proved more entertaining than the flight itself. Not a quitter, she finished her pilot's course and earned her commercial license and instrument rating.

Since then, she has traded in her wings for a keyboard where she lets her imagination soar to create fictional adventures that explore the power of love and the thrill of suspense. When not writing, she enjoys the outdoors with her husband and two children, quilt-making, photography and reading whatever catches her interest.

You can write to Sylvie at P.O. Box 702, Milford, NH 03055. And visit her Web site at www.sylviekurtz.com:

Books by Sylvie Kurtz

HARLEQUIN INTRIGUE
653—REMEMBERING RED THUNDER*
657—RED THUNDER RECKONING*
712—UNDER LOCK AND KEY
767—HEART OF A HUNTER**
773—MASK OF A HUNTER**
822—A ROSE AT MIDNIGHT
866—EYE OF A HUNTER**
872—PRIDE OF A HUNTER**
960—PULL OF THE MOON
1004—SPIRIT OF A HUNTER**

*Flesh and Blood
**The Seekers

CAST OF CHARACTERS

Sabriel Mercer—The Seeker knows how far Thomas Camden's reach extends.

Nora Picard Camden—The ex-deejay was once full of life, but to protect her son, she had to give up her independence. To get him back, she's willing to go to hell.

Thomas Prescott Camden III (The Colonel)—He's determined to control everyone in his world. He wants his grandson to carry on his legacy and is willing to kill whoever gets in his way.

Thomas Prescott Camden IV (Tommy)—His father's manipulation twisted his mind, and he's determined to save his son from a similar fate.

Thomas Prescott Camden V (Scotty)—He worships his father and would follow him anywhere, but his asthma could stop his flight short.

Melvyn Boggs—The experiment that corrupted Tommy's mind enhanced Boggs. No mission is too stressful. No task is too arduous. No environment is too harsh. Boggs follows orders without question.

Dane Hutt and Rod Costlow—Thomas's hired muscle.

Anna Camden Mercer—She was so determined to get away from her father's suffocating home that she drove herself to extremes.

Chapter One

Sabriel Mercer guarded the church's arched doorway, nodding curtly at each arriving guest, wishing he were anywhere but there. He rolled his shoulder against the starched stiffness of the rented tux and tugged at the noose-tight shirt collar with a finger. Only for a fellow Seeker would he endure such torture.

Church bells pealed, echoing with joy in Wintergreen's Currier-and-Ives town square. Indian summer spiked the air with warmth on this first weekend of October. With their explosion of gold and red, even the trees got in to the celebration.

A perfect day. His hands itched to plane the maple planks he'd joined for the kitchen cabinets of the cabin he was building. Instead, there he was holding a basket with a big cranberry bow. He wasn't sure what he'd done to deserve this public emasculation.

"Cell phone." Sabriel shoved the basket at Hale Harper, straggling in late, as usual. Rumor was Harper was Falconer's cousin, which would explain the slack Falconer cut him.

"It's off." Harper held the device up so Sabriel could verify his claim.

"Orders from the boss. Hand it over."

Harper glowered, his dark brows and eyes pinching much like Falconer's did when he wasn't pleased. "Falconer?"

"Liv."

Without another word Harper dropped his cell phone with the dozen already in the basket and made his way into the nave. There was no point arguing with Liv. Even the newest Seeker understood that Sebastian Falconer's wife always got her way.

Standing in the refuge of the vestibule, Sabriel scanned the crowd seated in the wooden pews. Most were strangers, people from the bride and groom's hometown in Massachusetts. With no desire to join the crush, he melded deeper into the shadows.

The organ overhead in the loft stopped its nasal whine midbar, then burst into "The Wedding March." The notes plucked at memories he'd thought he'd reconciled. But was there ever a way to explain a senseless death?

His jaw knotted. *Eyes ahead.*

On the arm of her former WITSEC inspector, Abrielle Holbrook glided down the aisle. She glowed in champagne silk. Sabriel knuckled the tender spot at his breastbone, grinding down until the serrated pain dulled. His wife had done that, too—chosen an off-white dress because she'd wanted to shine on her wedding day. She'd said that pure white made her look dead.

If only he'd known…. He shook his head and forced

himself to concentrate on Reed and Abbie's moment of happiness.

Grayson Reed looked as if he'd swallowed the sun as his bride made her way up the crimson carpet.

Noah Kingsley, Seekers, Inc.'s computer wiz, stood at Reed's side, red suspenders visible under the black tux that fit his compact body as if it had been made for him—and probably had.

Falconer and Liv, wrapped arm in arm, beamed at the bride.

The newly engaged Dominic Skyralov held hands, fingers twined with Luci Taylor. His other arm looped around her son's shoulders. There was a settled air about the blond cowboy that had been missing before he'd found Luci and Brendan. The corner of Sabriel's mouth twitched. Watching Skyralov play Mr. Mom when Luci started at the police academy next month was going to be a kick.

Sabriel squeezed his nape and the portrait of joy before him turned into mist. Had he ever been that happy? He couldn't remember. He'd thought so once. But his few months with Anna were nothing more than a dream, eclipsed by the nightmare that had followed. He'd barely survived the Colonel's revenge. But he'd kept Anna's secret.

A phone warbled a tinny melody. His? He frowned down at the pocket of his tuxedo jacket. Other than the Seekers gathered in this church, only his mother and Tommy had this number.

And neither would dial it unless he was their last recourse.

LAST NIGHT.

Tommy Camden had many faults, but the one quality he had in spades was patience.

In the cold of night, he squatted by the Camden estate's iron-and-stone fence, watching, waiting. He'd zapped the CCTV with a program to loop already filmed footage. His father had always underestimated him. Lack of military motivation didn't equal lack of brains.

Caesar and Brutus, the German shepherd guards, were chowing down on Benadryl-laced hunks of moose. Tommy had spent months priming them to override their training to be fed only by their handler—whose own free lunch had proved soporific. When he woke up, he wouldn't tell. Not if he wanted to keep his job. Tommy smirked. And where else was there to work in this butt-end-of-nowhere town except for the Camdens?

The balls of his feet were going numb and Tommy willed one more set of lights to blink out.

Nora had protected their son for the past ten years, but if the conversation Tommy had overheard on his last visitation with Scotty was already in motion, then Nora would soon be caged in a loony bin, drugged to the gills, so far off the map that Scotty wouldn't even appear in the margins. Then nothing would stand between the Colonel's cruel hand and Scotty.

Scotty was too good, too sweet to be broken. He should have a chance to make choices. He should get to laugh and play and be an ordinary kid.

Nora would understand. She always had—even when Tommy had betrayed her. She knew what the Colonel was capable of doing. She'd see that Tommy had to save their son from this circle of hell.

At precisely eleven, the Colonel's bedroom light snapped off, and Tommy leaked out the breath he hadn't even realized he'd held prisoner. Only the security spots lit the perimeter of the I-shaped English country estate. For all his unbending rhetoric on tradition and heritage, the Colonel had all but gutted the interior of the house after Grandpop's death eleven years ago. He'd modernized the gray stone house, with its slate roof and steeply pitched gables, to an inch of its original design—and destroyed everything that had comforted.

What would Grandpop think of what the Colonel had done to his grand old home? Or to his business?

Tommy shook his head. It didn't matter. None of it mattered. Only getting Scotty out before it was too late mattered.

Brutus groaned and stretched by the gate. Tommy petted the tan-and-black rump. "Sorry, boy, but I couldn't let you or your brother alert the Colonel. You'll both live to snarl another day."

Tommy stealed along the stone wall, a shadow among shadows, to the back of the mansion. He fished out a Maglite from his camouflage pants and signaled Scotty. The two quick flashes answering him told him Scotty was awake and ready—a gamble Tommy had hated to take.

Makes you just like the old man. Lie and cheat as long as it gets you what you want. Tommy shrugged away the guilt. Not the same thing. Not the same thing at all. The Colonel broke. *I'm trying to fix.*

Tommy had shown Scotty how to disarm the alarm system. Would he remember? Tommy had Scotty prepare an "adventure kit." Had he put everything in? Tommy had sworn the boy to secrecy—even from his mother. Had Scotty been able to keep their secret adventure from Nora? So many uncertainties. But Tommy had seen no other way around the Colonel's protective fortress.

He wished he could have taken Scotty during a visitation instead—cleaner, less dangerous. But two hours lead wasn't enough. Tomorrow being Saturday, he'd get at least eight, possibly ten. Long enough—if Nora understood the note.

The door to the back entry inched open. Pulse keeping jagged time, Tommy hoped that the Colonel's Glenlivet nightcap had put him under. Scotty's blond head poked through the door, and he looked left and right as if he were about to cross a street, then searched along the fence, into the darkness.

Tommy's gaze flickered to the bedroom windows. All black. His thumb hesitated on the Maglite's switch. *Last chance, Tommy. No going back if you give him the all-clear.*

With a guttural explosion of breath, Tommy signaled Scotty. Under the spots, Scotty's smile ate up his face. Red backpack flopping on his back, Scotty zipped across the manicured lawn. "Dad!"

"Shh!"

Scotty slapped a hand across his mouth and kept

running. He'd lucked into Nora's good brain and her laughing brown eyes, but had inherited Tommy's unruly blond curls and his lust for the outdoors.

Pride-swelled tears bruised Tommy's chest. God, he loved that boy. But love wasn't enough. He'd let him down so many times. With a flex of fingers, he tightened both hands into fists and rose to parade-review straightness. No more. He would do for Scotty what he couldn't do for himself: he'd set him free.

When Scotty reached the fence, Tommy lifted him, backpack and all—he was so light!—to the top of the stone wall, then changed his grip and helped him over the iron spikes.

As he checked his son over, as he looked into that innocent face, a chicken bone of breath lodged in Tommy's throat. What if he couldn't do this? What if he failed Scotty again? What if all he managed to do was lead his son into a deeper hell?

"Dad?"

Tommy forced a smile. "Hey, champ, are you ready for our big adventure?"

Brown eyes bright with anticipation, Scotty patted his backpack. "I got everything, just like you said."

Well, what's it going to be, Ranger? Action—or another excuse?

Rangers lead the way.

Tommy folded Scotty's small hand in his. Time to set a proper example for his son. *Be a man, Tommy.* He did an about-face on his past and focused on his mission. "Let's roll."

THIS MORNING.

"Hey, sleepyhead." Nora Camden pushed open Scotty's bedroom door and peeked in, anticipating her son's protesting grumbles. He wasn't a morning person.

Scotty had the covers up over his head, still hard asleep. He'd had a rough couple of days, and he'd desperately needed a decent night's sleep. She hated to wake him up, but the Colonel didn't have much patience with her interference or Scotty's asthma. He accused her of coddling the boy and making Scotty weak. As if a child could will himself well. As if a mother could watch her son suffer without doing everything she could to help him.

"It's almost nine." Nora added a lilt to her voice, hoping to lure Scotty out of hiding. "I talked the cook into letting me make some of your favorite blueberry pancakes. They're waiting for you in the kitchen. Come on. Up and at 'em."

No movement from the bed. "Scotty?" Had his asthma flared up again? How could she not have heard? Heart knocking, she rushed across the golden oak floorboards. "Did you have a bad night, sweetie? Why didn't you wake me up?"

She reached down to shake her son awake. Her hands sank into the lump on the bed and a gasp sucked all of the room's air into her lungs. She whipped off the denim comforter and found a fleece blanket vaguely shaped like a body. "This isn't funny, Scotty."

She dropped to her knees and skimmed a glance

under the bed. "I know you don't want to go to James Enger's party, but that's no reason to hide from me."

Another of the Colonel's attempts to get Scotty to fit in to the proper social circles. She snorted. As if offering up his grandson as prey to a bully would win anyone anything. Unfortunately, Nora had to weigh her battles and, on this one, she'd retreated.

She dusted off the knees of her black wool slacks— *Camden women are always proper, Nora*—and tilted her head at the closet door standing ajar. Scotty liked to hide there to read forbidden comic books with a flashlight. She pressed a hand to her mouth to stifle her amusement at his act of civil disobedience. "You don't have to stay long. I promise. We'll go late and, as soon as you've had cake, you can call, and I'll pick you right up."

She jerked open the closet door. Empty. Frowning, hands on hips, she whirled toward the center of the room. "Come on, Scotty. It's time to come out."

Where would he have gone? It wasn't as if he could leave the grounds. Not with the dogs and the alarm system ready to betray any attempt at escape. Even in this 13,000-square-foot house, there weren't that many places to hide from the Colonel's all-seeing eyes.

Maybe he'd sneaked into the family room for some cartoons. He'd better hope the Colonel didn't catch him or he'd have to endure another lecture on mass media's corrupting influence.

Nora's lips quivered into a smile. On the other hand, maybe that had been Scotty's plan all along. A lecture would make them even later for James's party, and

Scotty really hated James Enger. The Colonel didn't give the boy enough credit for smarts. She turned and headed out of the room.

That's when she spotted the note on Scotty's desk.

Nora—
Don't worry. Scotty's safe. We're going on an adventure—taking the Band on the Run on Route 66 to Deep Water and into Graceland. Talking Heads: 77.
Love, Tommy.

After his name, he'd doodled a smiling stick moose with giant antlers.

"Oh, Tommy, what have you done?" Why had he taken Scotty when he had visitation this afternoon? Was he off his meds?

She closed her eyes and squeezed the note tight. If she told the Colonel, he'd find Scotty, but Tommy would lose his visitations, and those visitations were what kept her ex-husband sane. And she didn't want Scotty to grow up not knowing his father. A child needed to know both his parents loved him. A child needed his family.

Her knees lost their locking ability and she sank onto the desk chair. Tommy was trying to tell her something with this note, but what? She ironed the piece of paper on the desk with the side of her fist until it was perfectly flat again. In spite of everything, Tommy adored their son. He wouldn't hurt Scotty. But if Tommy was off his bipolar disorder meds, he could be unpredictable. A pick of ice stabbed her heart. Would he be able to take care of Scotty then? What if Scotty had another asthma attack?

She bolted to Scotty's night table and rifled through the drawer. Scotty's inhaler was missing, but the disc of Advair was still there. She splayed a hand across her chest. "How could you do this, Tommy?"

Don't panic. Not yet. Scotty had his inhaler. He was due for a new one soon, but this one should last a couple of days. And he would be okay without the other meds for a day. Swallowing hard, she clenched the purple disc. He had to. *Please, please, don't let him have another big attack.*

"How could you? How could you? How could you?" Gritting her teeth, she searched Scotty's room for what was missing. His red backpack. His yellow fleece jacket. His camouflage pants. His hiking boots. Tiny bits of armor that would have to protect her son in whatever shortsighted foolishness Tommy had led him into. She batted at the runaway tears.

Tommy had put her in a sticky spot. But maybe she could rescue both father and son from the Colonel's sure punishment. She had to stall. Buy them time.

And find them both. The sooner, the better.

Back at the desk, she rubbed at the writing on the note as if it were a magic lamp. Tommy had given her the map. All she had to do was figure out the key to his insanity.

Scotty's okay. He's with his father who loves him. Everything will be okay.

She hung on to that thought and let it pulse a backbeat as she tried to decipher Tommy's code.

"Band on the Run" by Wings. She plunked her elbows on the desk and raked her hands through her hair. *Think! What does it mean?* Did he want her to focus on the title or were the lyrics part of the key? Was he running with someone else? Why was he running in the first place?

She dug her fingers into her scalp. "Route 66" by Bobby Troup. Was he really taking Route 66 or was he going two thousand miles or was it the kicks part she was supposed to make something out of?

"Deep Water" by Richard Clapton. She rubbed the heels of her palms against her pulsing temples. Was he drunk? Heading to California?

She fisted both hands into her hair and pulled. What was it with all the road songs? None of this made sense. *Tommy, help me out.*

"Where's the boy?"

Nora started and spun the desk chair around, instinctively blocking the note from the Colonel's view. He stood in the doorway, suit-clad body army-straight and stiff, white hair—what was left of it—cut military-short around the shiny pink dome, brown mustache and eyebrows accent marks on an already well-punctuated face.

"I thought he was with you." Of course her treacherous cheeks had to blush, giving away her lie. "You shouldn't force him to go to a party he doesn't want to attend."

The Colonel's nostrils flared at her inappropriate challenge. "James Enger is a fine, upstanding young man with a bright future ahead of him. It's never too early to make connections."

She knitted her hands in her lap to keep them from fidgeting like a nervous recruit. "I'm sure Scotty's around somewhere. He wouldn't want to disappoint you."

"I want him dressed and ready to go in ten minutes." The unspoken *or else* hung in the air.

"Yes, sir."

Shoot. What was she supposed to do now? Give Tommy up? No, not yet. There was still time to keep the peace.

As the Colonel left, she whipped back to the note. A fist of panic gripped her chest. *You can work through this, Nora.* Deep River. Maybe Tommy had taken Scotty for a hike along the Flint River. They loved to hike together, but two hours of visitation every other Saturday didn't give them much time. Not that she wanted Scotty stuck on the side of a hiking trail while having an asthma attack.

She shook her head. *Don't go to the worst-case scenario. Find them. Bring them home.* She dashed to her room, slipped the note, Scotty's Advair and a fresh inhaler in her purse, then headed toward the garage. Her lips disappeared into her mouth as she listened for the Colonel and tiptoed along the precisely cut diagonal limestone tiles in the hallway.

She was reaching for the key to her Mercedes on the pegboard by the garage door when the Colonel marched into the hall, steps thundering.

"Where's the boy?" he asked.

"Scotty's already in the car. I, uh, had to go back for something. We're heading off to the party. As ordered." Shoot, her face was flaming again.

The Colonel waved an envelope. "He forgot James's present."

"I'll take it." She reached out for the check.

The Colonel jammed it in his breast pocket. "I'm driving."

Double shoot. The Colonel stepped past her, the drumming heels of his boots a reminder of his power, and into the garage where half a dozen cars were parked. "Where is he?"

"In my car."

Oh, great, now she'd have to make Scotty look like an ungrateful grandchild to cover her lie. She pretended to look in the backseat, then under the car. "Scotty? Come out right now!"

"You need to keep a tighter hand on that child. A boy needs to know who's in charge. All this lack of discipline leads to insubordination."

"He's just a boy."

"He's a Camden. He has obligations. A reputation to uphold." Blocking her escape with his broad shoulders, the Colonel flipped open his cell phone and pressed a speed-dial button. "Prescott is missing."

Nora bit the tip of her tongue to keep herself from pleading Scotty's case. That would only make things worse. *Choose your battles.* Better to wait until she'd found him.

The Colonel's already ramrod-straight body stiffened. "I'll take care of it. Find the boy. Bring him to me."

Siccing hired muscle after a ten-year-old boy. Her fingers clenched around the strap of her purse. What was wrong with him? The bruiser would find Scotty all right, scare the snot out of him, then hand him to the Colonel. And the Colonel would feel obliged to punish Scotty for his unsoldier-like behavior. She couldn't let that happen.

Breathing in courage, she shored up her defenses. The thug might be good at tracking, but Scotty was her son, and she understood how his mind worked—and Tommy's, too, as fried as it was. The muscle would scour the estate, but she already knew Scotty and Tommy were gone. Key tight in hand, she wended her way around the Colonel's Cadillac toward her car.

"Where do you think you're going?" the Colonel barked at her.

"For a ride."

"Now?"

"I need fresh air." In spite of her best effort for a show of strength, she squirmed into position behind the wheel and reached for the armor of the door.

The Colonel grasped the top of it in one hand and denied her a shield. The pointed end of his icy stare pinned her against the blood-red leather upholstery. He knew. She swallowed the series of hard knots notching her throat. He knew she was holding something back. He knew that she wasn't telling the truth.

"If you're abetting Tommy's folly, you'll pay the price."

"I don't know what you mean."

"You lost the boy." In the cavernous garage, the Colonel's voice rumbled in warning.

"He isn't lost." *He's with his father.*

The Colonel's gaze slitted to a knife edge. If she

wasn't careful, she'd end up filleted. "I don't want you anywhere near that boy until I've had a talk with him about responsibility."

More like a hazing. A snort escaped her. "He's not a soldier. He's a little boy."

"He's a Camden."

Reminding her once again that only his benevolence allowed her to stay at the mansion. But what choice did she have? Scotty had never signed on for this tour of duty. If she tried to leave, the Colonel would use all of his influence to take her son away from her. The threat of loss ripped through her, leaving her clutching the edges of her seat to keep balanced. At least this way, she had a say. She could protect her son—the way Tommy's mother never had. The way her mother never had.

Nerves rattling, she ratcheted her chin up one notch…two. "I know where he likes to go when he's scared."

The Colonel's face quivered in a purple mottle. "You've turned him into a sissy boy."

I've made him into a sweet, mostly happy boy. Knowing her chances of searching for Scotty depended on the Colonel's goodwill, she submissively lowered her head. "I'll bring him home."

"See that you do."

With a shaky hand, Nora cranked the engine over and backed out of the garage bay. She stopped at the gate and waited for the iron monstrosity to lumber open.

The situation was getting worse. Every year the Colonel expected more out of Scotty, and his expectations were beyond Scotty's age capacity, especially with the asthma factored in.

She had to get her son out. Somehow. She had to find a way. But how? A sea of tears formed in her chest, swirled into a hurricane and threatened the back of her eyes with landfall. Dumpster-diving for food was no life for a sick boy. How could she get him the medicine he needed, the education he deserved, the safe home every child should have?

The Colonel would never stop looking for them. She blinked against the coming storm of tears. He'd made that immensely clear after she'd had the nerve to divorce Tommy. And he'd follow up on his threats. Scotty was his only grandchild. His only heir now that he'd disowned Tommy. He had the resources—money, influence, power.

Her mouth opened, greedy for air. And she had nothing. No money, no family, no job.

She'd seen him break more than one person to get what he wanted—starting with his own wife and children. She couldn't leave Scotty alone to be raised by such a hard man.

She rolled through the gate and shuddered. Once past the corner of the property, the concrete holding her shoulders stiff and high cracked, releasing them, and her breathing became freer. She'd often wondered if Scotty's asthma was related more to the caustic air in the mansion than to inflamed lungs.

At the stop at the end of Camden Road, she hesitated, her foot tap, tapping the brakes. *Tommy, where are you?*

Band on the Run. Route 66. Deep Water. Graceland. Talking Heads: 77. What are you trying to say?

The blast of a horn behind her jolted her in her seat. She signaled a right and, after checking both ways, turned. She searched all the places Tommy liked to take Scotty. The ice-cream parlor on Juniper Street. The school playground off Red Barn Road. The pet store on Woodpecker Lane.

By lunchtime, she'd looked in every park and playground of Camden, at every trailhead, at every boat ramp, and she hadn't spotted Tommy's battered Jeep. He wasn't answering his cell phone and, according to his boss, he'd cashed in his two weeks of vacation time.

What if, as the titles suggested, he'd run? Ice doused her veins. No, he wouldn't do that, not knowing how much it would hurt her. He'd have included her in any escape plan. He knew Scotty was her life.

Unless.

The rock of her heart sank to her shoes and a cold sweat soaked her through.

Hadn't Tommy said that the Colonel had first shipped him out to military boarding school at eleven? And military school hadn't suited Tommy—just as it wouldn't suit Scotty. If he was off his meds, then Tommy could become fixated on saving Scotty.

Cold seeped into her bones, clacked her teeth. What if he *was* headed to California and planned to hide with Scotty—as far away from the Colonel as he could get?

You should have talked to me, Tommy. The Colonel and I have an agreement. No boarding schools. Ever.

Bent over the steering wheel, peering out the windshield for any sign of her son, she inched on White Mountain Road along the Flint River. She cranked up the heat and the radio. She wasn't panicked. Not yet. "Tommy, please help me."

"Burning Down the House" by the Talking Heads blasted over the speakers. Her brain fired with a bright light, and she bobbled the steering wheel, lurching toward the rain-swollen river. She jammed on the brakes, crunching on the shoulder's gravel, and part of Tommy's message became clear. "Oh, no, Tommy. What have you done?"

Chapter Two

Nora braked to a halt on the gravel shoulder. On the other side of the car, the Flint River pulsed and pounded over its rocky bottom in perfect imitation of Nora's gushing thoughts.

Talking in code had been the only way to communicate certain things while living under the Colonel's prying eyes. Talking Heads—telephone. 77—the last two digits of the emergency number Tommy had given her in one of his delusional phases. Her hands shook on the steering wheel, and she gripped it harder.

If you're ever in trouble, Nora, Tommy had said, instructing her to memorize the number in blue ink he printed on her forearm. *Call this number. Next to you, Sabriel's the only person in the world I trust. He'll help you. He owes me.*

Sabriel Mercer. Tommy's best friend. Anna's husband. One of the unfortunate victims of the Colonel's vengeful bent. He'd been Tommy's best man at their wedding. That was the one and only time she'd met him. They'd barely exchanged more than a few words. She couldn't even bring up a clear picture of the man other than dark and brooding—a little scary, actually, with those feral green eyes peering out of the shadows of the room. The ex-Ranger seemed alone even in the roomful of acquaintances Tommy had gathered to witness their exchange of vows—an event unsanctioned by the Colonel. She'd had no idea the flak that would cause once he heard the news.

She didn't know much else about Sabriel Mercer, except that something had happened to him and Tommy at Ranger School, something that Tommy would never talk about. Something that had changed them both.

And if Tommy was asking her to call Sabriel Mercer for help, something was terribly wrong.

The mountains spread out in front of her in an endless vista. The rusty blanket of dying autumn leaves faded to blue and purple in the distance. Centuries of wind and rain had sculpted the granite and trees. Those mountains were both an awe-inspiring beauty and a treacherous territory that swallowed up hikers like sacrificial offerings. They were the only place Tommy had ever felt at home. The only place his broken spirit could rest.

A sinking feeling weighed her down into the seat, making it impossible to breathe. Band on the Run. Like he had that summer with Sabriel when they were fifteen? If he'd sought refuge in the mountains, then she would never find him, and the Colonel would win. Scotty would lose his father, and she would lose another foothold in directing Scotty's upbringing.

Her chest stuttered. She couldn't do this. She couldn't go into those mountains and hope to find her son. Not alone. She didn't even know where to start.

But Sabriel would.

The tightness holding her breath hostage released a finger of its hold. Sabriel had wandered those mountains with Tommy. He might know what Route 66, Deep Water and Graceland stood for. He'd know where to look. He'd know where to find Tommy before the Colonel's trackers did. And if she brought Scotty home instead of the hired muscle, then the Colonel would have to respect the status quo.

The tires squealed as Nora pulled a U-turn in the middle of White Mountain Road and pointed the car toward Camden. She'd grown paranoid over the years and was sure the Colonel somehow monitored her cell phone as well as her social calendar and her food intake. After all, she was a Camden and Camdens were expected to behave in a certain manner.

She piloted the car to the local gas station—a lowly place the Colonel would never frequent—and parked in front of the convenience store. The crazed *ding-ding-ding* of the open car door chased her to the pay phone. The expectant hiss of the receiver added to the static of her mind. Squeezing her eyes closed, she brought up the image of Tommy inking Sabriel's number on her forearm. She fed coins into the machine, dialed and waited, biting her lower lip, while the number rang and rang and rang.

"Mercer."

Nora jumped at the terse sound of the voice. "Tommy's friend?"

"Who's asking?"

"Nora Camden." She wriggled her body until she faced the parking lot and Main Street, scanning both for signs of the Colonel's men. "Tommy told me that if I was ever in trouble, I should call this number."

Silence. Had the line died? "Mr. Mercer?"

"Are you in trouble?"

She scraped her fingernails along her scalp, pulling her hair tight when she reached the crown of her head. "Yes. No. I mean, Tommy's in trouble." She puffed out a breath. "He took our son. If the Colonel finds him before I do, he'll take Scotty away from me, and he'll deny Tommy visitations forever. You know how the Colonel is. No give. Those visitations mean the world to Tommy. He needs them as much as Scotty."

More deafening silence.

Nora cradled the receiver with both hands. "Mr. Mercer? Are you there? If Tommy's off his meds, then Scotty could be in danger, too."

Still no response. But in the background, a voice intoned some sort of incantation.

"Scotty has asthma," Nora continued, compelled to plead her case. Surely Sabriel wouldn't be heartless enough to let a sick boy die. "He left with an inhaler that's almost empty. I need to get his medicine to him. If he has an attack out there, he could die."

Her top teeth sank into her bottom lip and drew blood. He doesn't care. Tommy was wrong. Sabriel wasn't going to pay his debt. She blinked back the tears scoring at her eyes. "I think he's planning on hiding Scotty from the Colonel. I think he thinks he's helping Scotty. I think he's gone into the mountains."

"Was there a note?"

"Yes."

"Read everything on the paper."

She did, even describing the drawing of the moose.

"I'll find him," Sabriel said with a certainty she envied.

"I'm coming with you."

"No."

"Scotty needs his medicine. It's cold out there, and cold is one of his triggers." So was anxiety. She couldn't help the desperation crowding her voice.

"I work alone."

"Do you know what it's like to not be able to breathe? He's just a little boy, and those attacks scare him."

Her body straightened against the hard skeleton of the phone cubicle. She was going with him. She needed to know Scotty was all right. She had to get Sabriel to come to her.

A cheer erupted in the background, drowning out Sabriel's nerve-shredding silence.

"I can't go back to the estate," Nora continued, voice strong with resolve. "Not without Scotty. The Colonel'll use my failure as ammunition to take more control over Scotty. I can't let that happen. I can't let him turn Scotty into another Tommy." She flinched at the put-down of her ex-husband. She wasn't the manipulative type. At least not usually. But if she didn't stand up for Scotty, who would?

"Where are you?" Sabriel finally asked.

For the first time since she'd found the note, a sense of hope rose up to calm her. She was not alone. Somebody understood. Somebody would help her find Scotty. "I'm at a pay phone at a gas station in Camden."

"Were you followed?"

Her gaze darted and flitted at the passing traffic on Main Street. Pickup trucks, SUVs and beaters in various stages of decomposition trundled by, but no black Hummer like those driven by the Colonel's security staff. "I don't think so."

"Do you know where Black Swan Lake is?"

"North of Camden. But he's not there. I've already checked the boat ramps."

"There's a camp on the west side of the lake. The Lemire Adventure Camp."

Could finding him really be that easy? A pressure valve of release sagged her against the phone. "You think that's where Tommy went?"

"No. A friend of mine runs it. I'll meet you there."

"How long will it take you to get to the camp?"

"An hour."

An hour was a lifetime when you couldn't breathe. "How long before you can find them?"

"Depends on their head start."

The small thread of hope unraveled. She had no idea what time they'd left the estate. Would Tommy have made Scotty hike in the dark? That sounded so dangerous. How far could he get with a ten-year-old in tow?

The pulse of time running out ticked much too loudly

in her brain. *Find him. Find Scotty. Find him now.* Today. Before night fell again. Night always made Scotty's symptoms worse. "Hurry."

SABRIEL CORNERED Falconer as he was leaving the church. Departing guests created a buzz that wavered through the high-ceilinged vestibule and grated against Sabriel's already raw nerves. "I need some time off."

Falconer hiked an eyebrow in question.

"Personal," Sabriel said.

Although Falconer knew about Ranger School, about Anna, about the Colonel, Sabriel's fingers twitched on the live wire of his shame. He couldn't hide anything that was on record from the man who'd given him more than one second chance. But Falconer didn't know about Tommy or the experiment gone wrong. Or the pact they'd made at fifteen to always watch each other's backs.

Sabriel couldn't let Tommy charge into a suicide mission. The Colonel was too strong for the broken man his friend had become. And Nora was right. He couldn't allow the Colonel to turn Scotty into another Tommy. He owed his friend that much.

Falconer grinned. "Trying to get out of the reception?"

Sabriel shook his head, though missing the shindig would be a bonus. Answering the same curious questions about his mixed heritage made him feel like a gorilla in a cage. He loved every branch of his crazy family tree—Japanese, Irish, Abenaki and French Canadian. He just didn't like discussing them.

"Everything okay with the family?" Falconer asked as if he'd been reading his mind.

"Something I have to take care of."

Falconer's eyebrows met in the center of his forehead. "How much time?"

"A week, tops. Harper can take the lead on the Carter case. Smuggling's up his alley."

"You haven't missed a single day of work since you signed up with Seekers eight months ago. Not even after you broke your wrist and ankle tracking the piece of garbage who tried to kill Liv. Or when you were with the Marshals Service."

Falconer's keen gaze sliced into him, jabbing past the tough skin to the tender organs. Sabriel stood unmoving, gaze locked with Falconer's, unflinching. Time off would have given him too much time to think. And some questions, he'd discovered, shouldn't be answered.

"You're overdue," Falconer said.

Sabriel nodded once, relief calmed his juiced muscles.

"If there's anything we can do," Falconer said, "we're here for you."

The rest of the Seekers would stand by him, though he'd never given them a reason to. And that counted for more than he could admit out loud. Though he was loathe to ask for a favor, with the Colonel involved, Nora could be in danger. "A friend might need a safe house."

"Call."

Sabriel nodded, thankful Seekers had found him and given a purpose to his empty days. He cast a glance Reed and Abbie's way, and a flash of Anna—head thrown back, laughing—leaked out of its locked memory box. Frowning, he squeezed it back in. "Give them my apologies."

"I will." Falconer's curious gaze followed him out of the church, but Sabriel dismissed it. Falconer would give him space—no questions asked. That trust was why Sabriel was still at Seekers.

He pulled into the dirt drive leading to his half-finished log cabin in Harrisville in less than fifteen minutes. A record, even for him. He changed into hiking gear and grabbed the rucksack he kept at the ready.

Wait for me, Anna. The remembered plea in his voice was smoke in his brain. A slap of nausea rammed his shoulder into the wall, stopping his mad dash, leaving him panting. Anna, studying the sea, appeared on the screen of his mind. Her long blond hair whipped over her face in a silky veil. Always a little part of her hidden from him, just out of reach…

"*I'll be there tomorrow.*"

"*There's a storm coming in,*" she said, and he could hear tight despair in her voice. "*I need to get the dive in before the rain hits. The sponsors—*"

"*Can damn well wait. I'm your safety diver.*"

"*I've got a whole crew to take care of me.*"

The nausea swelled, lacing his throat with acid.

This wasn't Anna. He wasn't half a world away. He'd get to Tommy in time.

Don't think. Don't feel. Just do.

Swallowing down the bitter bile, he pushed himself off the wall. From a temporary metal pantry he extracted enough freeze-dried meals to last a week. As he filled his water bladder, his thoughts drifted to Nora's call.

He couldn't place the fear-sharpened voice on the phone with the beaming face of the woman who'd walked down the aisle on Tommy's arm and made him look happier than Sabriel had ever seen him. Watching Nora spin around the dance floor with Tommy, her brown hair with its golden light flying around her, her bright laughter more melodious than the music playing in the background, Sabriel could see why Tommy had fallen for her, and he'd been glad for his friend. And when he'd noticed the old-soul scars in Nora's golden-brown eyes, he'd wished them both the happiness they deserved.

Sabriel stashed the water bladder in its rucksack pocket. He knew about Scotty, knew about the divorce, knew about the peace Tommy had found as an outfitter for a local resort from yearly birthday e-mails. But they hadn't talked to each other since the wedding. Too much pain. Too much guilt.

He booted up the computer in search of a weather update and a bird's-eye view of the mountains. Snow wasn't unheard of at this time of the year, and he wanted to be prepared. The rain had broken, for now, but another wave was due by the end of the week. How long could it take to track down Tommy? No more than a day or two. The kid had to slow him down.

Sabriel figured that Tommy had gone to one of three places—Goose Neck Mountain, Mount Storm or Pilgrim's Peak. But if Tommy was smart, he'd avoid the obvious and head for new territory. The Colonel still had trackers at his bellow, and like an elephant, he never forgot. The mountains would be the first place he'd look for Tommy, especially Mount Storm, where his trackers had found them at the end of their stolen summer.

Clicking over to the White Mountain National Forest site, Sabriel wondered for the millionth time what he could have done differently. As always, the stack of possibilities clashed against a blank wall of reality.

He forced himself to focus on the loading Web page. Heavy rain in the past week had swollen streams and saturated the soil. Water crossings, trails and gravel roads could be difficult or dangerous to negotiate, according to the hiker's warning on the home page.

Was Tommy off his meds? Was his judgment impaired? Taking a sick kid on such a rough hike, what was he thinking?

The only way to know Tommy's ultimate destination was to follow the clues he'd left behind. The Smiling Moose was a café halfway between Camden and I-93. 66 was 6.6 miles past the café to the trailhead off White Mountain Road where the Flint River took a sharp jog out of the mountains. And Graceland was the whole damned White Mountain National Forest—780,000 acres of pure wilderness.

Sabriel loaded his biodiesel-powered Jeep and smiled at the memory of Tommy at fifteen, so eager to be free. When Will Daigle—the mountain man who'd taught him and Tommy to survive invisibly in the mountains—had told them about the songlines many ancient navigators used to orient themselves, Tommy had mistaken the meaning and fallen back on his vast knowledge of music to keep track of his place in the woods. Their shared joke would help keep the Colonel's men stranded for a while. That should give Sabriel a chance to find Tommy before he got himself killed.

But just because he was willing to trek after Tommy, didn't mean he'd let an inexperienced hiker tag along. Nora would slow him down and speed was of the essence. He'd get the kid's medicine, make her see that he'd get to Tommy faster if he tracked alone, then stash her at the Aerie—Seekers, Inc.'s headquarters—where Falconer and Liv could keep an eye on her.

He pocketed his cell phone, a hunting knife and, as an afterthought, climbed to the loft and retrieved the 9mm Beretta he'd stashed in a locker beneath the camp cot. He turned the weapon over in his hand, heavy with potentiality, black like death.

Once when Sabriel was twelve, he'd complained to Grandpa Yamawashi that he couldn't hold his ground against his bigger, stronger brothers, and wished he had a gun or a knife to up his odds. Grandpa had said, "The greatest warrior is one who never has to use his sword."

In the Army, an unspoken but understood position was that the winner carried the bigger gun. The Colonel and his men lived by that belief. Risking a showdown unarmed was suicide.

And as much as guilt was a noose around his conscience, he wanted to face death on his terms, not the Colonel's.

Sabriel holstered the pistol and strapped it on. The alien weight jarred his gait. He added two extra fifteen-round magazines to his rucksack, fervently hoping he'd find Tommy before he had to draw.

THOMAS PRESCOTT CAMDEN III stood at the window of his office and surveyed his realm. His chest puffed up at the sense of history and achievement spread out before him. Generations had turned this parcel of rocky land into a showpiece, with its artful gardens, manicured lawn and hand-stacked granite wall.

One fist balled at his side.

What an ungrateful grandson he had. How could he turn his back on all the advantages that had been laid at his feet? Didn't he know men would kill for what was handed to him on a golden platter?

Nora's fault, of course. She was too soft on the boy, always coddling him, petting him, hugging him. How was the boy supposed to grow a spine that way?

Thomas, like all Camdens, had been raised in a heritage of ambition, success and expectations. Camden men went to West Point. Camden men joined the Army and shone through Ranger school. Camden men retired from stellar military service to their country after twenty years, then, with pride, took over the helm of Camden Laboratories, and continued their service to their brothers at arms by developing products and supplements that would ease a soldier's hard life.

Camden men had founded this town—which bore their name—over a hundred years ago. There they were kings, respected by all. Producing a male heir to follow in their footsteps was a Camden man's duty and honor.

Thomas had followed the preordained path. He'd lived up to and surpassed every expectation. He'd done everything right.

A too-familiar rumble growled in his chest. To have his son prove a failure and his daughter die before she could give him a grandson was hard enough to take. But to have this *woman*—a street urchin, no less—ruin his last chance to pass on his legacy galled him to no end.

She'd destroyed Tommy's bright future, and now she was using Tommy to steal away his only grandchild. The balled fist rattled the window frame. He refused to let her win this battle.

His narrowed gaze zeroed in on the bronze of the original Thomas Prescott Camden, sword raised in victory, and Thomas's fist unclenched.

The boy's weakness would disappear once his smothering mother was out of the way. All the boy needed was a firm hand, the right training, some toughening up. There was still time to save him from Tommy's unfortunate fate. Tommy had failed because of his own feckless character, not because of a transfer of defective genes.

And Anna? What else could you expect from a woman? They weren't meant for the battlefield of business. That she'd crumpled at the first sign of conflict wasn't a surprise. It was his error in judgment for thinking that Camden blood made her different.

As for Nora, she needed to learn that, when it came

to Camden family business, his word was law. She'd defied him for the last time.

Thomas spun on a perfectly polished heel to face Melvyn Boggs, who stood at attention before the original Colonel's desk. Boggs was his greatest success story. Thomas had handpicked him right out of Ranger School—the same class his son had failed so miserably.

At thirty-six the soldier's body was harder and fitter than most men a decade younger in this spoiled generation. Only the lean, sun-baked face betrayed the hours of training in the harsh elements. The man had nerves of steel and a mind as sharp as the keenest of blades. The experiment that had corrupted Tommy's gray matter had enhanced Boggs's fine instrument. No mission was too stressful. No task too arduous. No environment too severe. Boggs would follow orders without question.

"Find her," Thomas said. "Make sure she has an accident. Then bring the boy back to me. Unharmed."

Thomas strode to the wall-mounted topographical map of the area and circled Mount Storm with his index finger. "This is where Tommy's headed."

People tended to follow the path of least resistance. In moments of stress, they turned to points of comfort. And for Tommy that was the mountains. Even in this vast area, Tommy—like the animal he'd become—had staked out territory over the years. He'd track through familiar trails, and an ace like Boggs would have no trouble following his trace.

"What about Tommy?" Boggs asked.

Tommy was a failure beyond redemption. "Put him out of his misery."

Chapter Three

The discreet hand-carved wooden sign announced the Lemire Adventure Camp and promised women the opportunity to learn outdoor skills with like-minded sisters.

Maybe Nora didn't need a hero after all. Maybe these outdoorswomen would guide her through the mountains to track down Scotty. Sure beat waiting around.

The cinnamon gum she'd popped to calm the sea of acid swirling in her stomach turned to modeling clay in her mouth.

She discarded the gum into the ashtray and the car's clock flashed over another precious minute. Where was Scotty now? How much farther away from home? How many minutes could she waste and still find him alive and well?

A rusty chain barred the gravel drive. Her heart tip-tapped with uncertainty. Was she supposed to wait there or drive on up? Sabriel should have given her better instructions. Didn't he know the stakes? Didn't he know that one mistake could take her son away from her forever?

Breathe, Nora. She forced in a breath and streamed it out in one long run, tamping back the frayed edge of her anxiety. *Hold yourself together. You won't help Scotty by going ballistic.*

Logic. A plan. That would help her find Scotty, not blind panic. Her gaze slid through the car's mirrors. Her white boat of a car would make too big a target on the narrow lane. She couldn't park there.

She unclamped her stiff finger from the steering wheel, shoved open the door and unhooked the chain. She drove through, then stared at the heavy links in her hands. Should she hook the chain back up or leave it down? What did it say about the state of her mind that simple decisions required a Herculean effort?

This was all Tommy's fault. Why did he have to take Scotty? Maybe everything wasn't perfect at the estate, but they were safe.

She dropped the chain with a snort of disgust and let it lie like a dead boa constrictor. Leaving it down would save Sabriel time, and they could get going faster.

Back in the car, her gaze flitted from the thick pines lining the winding gravel drive to the shadows shifting like black ghouls searching to devour light. One thing was sure: the Colonel would never find her there. And that gave her a measure of confidence.

At the top of the drive, half a dozen cabins that looked too rustic to provide comfort or fun flanked a main lodge with a green roof and time-silvered logs. She parked by the hitching post to the left of the lodge.

The place looked deserted, and the oppressive quiet

pressed on her chest, making her want to scream at the world. *Stop it, stop it, stop it!* How could the earth keep turning, the birds singing, the water lapping when Scotty was missing? She wrapped her arms over her chest, feeling the void of her son's small body.

As she took in the scene, she realized Scotty would have loved it there—the woods to explore, the lake to swim, the campfire to tell stories. Tommy had talked about taking Scotty camping overnight last summer. But the Colonel had stamped the request "refused."

"Why is the Colonel so mean?" Scotty had asked, pouting.

Nora had no answer. Not then. Not now.

As her gaze searched the grounds, she wrung her hands in her lap. Where were the outdoorswomen? Wasn't someone supposed to meet her? There were no other vehicles. No voices. Nothing. No one.

She couldn't just sit there and wait. She'd go crazy.

Clothes. You need outdoor clothes. Sabriel would arrive soon. And if she was ready, he'd have to take her to the mountains and help her find Scotty.

She rammed the car door open and headed for the lodge. Away from the car's heater, the air chilled her through her sweater down to the skin. Her knock on the lodge door brought only a fading echo.

She curved a hand to the window and peeked through the glass. No movement. "Hello? Anybody there?"

The stubborn knob resisted her attempts to turn it. Was the camp closed for the winter? Why hadn't Sabriel mentioned he was sending her to a deserted place?

On the other side of the hitching post, two A-frames groaned under the burden of red kayaks—three on each side. The grating ratchetlike calls of blue jays in a nearby oak jangled her already frazzled nerves. With halting footsteps she followed the path through the trees that would lead her to the cottages. Maybe all the Amazons were out hiking. Maybe they'd left some spare clothes behind.

The trail curved around a narrow strip of beach. The cloud-leached sun eked out pale light that barely scratched at the surface of the water. Pulling out her cell phone, she paced the length of a bench made from a fallen log placed around the dead fire in the stone pit. She was too worried to care if the Colonel had access to her call records. Biting her lower lip, she listened to the incessant ringing of Tommy's phone.

She growled when Tommy's voice mail kicked on. "Tommy, *please*. Call me. I need to know Scotty's okay."

How many messages had she left him? At least a dozen. What if something had happened? What if that was why Tommy hadn't called to reassure her?

Scotty's with his father, who loves him, she reminded herself for the thousandth time. It wasn't as if a stranger had kidnapped him and was holding him for ransom in some dark hole. Tommy wouldn't let any harm come to their son.

Unless Tommy was off his meds.

Her hand strangled the phone and she gulped in air. Scotty was fine. Tommy was fine. They were both perfectly fine. To think otherwise would push her over the brink into insanity. And she couldn't afford that. Scotty was depending on her.

The mountains loomed on the other side of the lake, taunting her with their nearness, with her helplessness to find one little boy in their midst.

She slammed the phone shut. There was no one else to call. No Amazons to the rescue. Only Sabriel.

Adrenaline ants scurried through her limbs, goading her to take action. With an irrationality bordering on mania, she wanted to turn over rocks, climb trees, ford rivers—anything to find Scotty. She whirled away from the tormenting mountains and jogged toward the cabins.

Fingers of wind rustled through the fallen leaves in the woods and reminded her of chattering teeth. The shifting shadows of trees creeped her out—as if eyes were watching her from behind every trunk, following her, waiting to pounce. She half expected a pack of rabid wolves, yellow teeth bared, red tongues lolling, fiery eyes glowing, to spring out at her. Never mind that there weren't any wolves in these parts.

Her pace faltered. Oh, God, what if Tommy and Scotty were attacked by a bear? Or charged by a moose? Or pounced on by a bobcat?

Up ahead, a cottage creaked. The haunting wail of its misery lingered in the brittle air. Nora froze. Her breath chugged in ragged bursts.

"Hello?" Her voice fractured like a teen scream-queen's. "Is anyone there?"

No answer but the lamenting sough of wind.

Her gaze scoured the woods. Never before had she felt so isolated. Alone like this, she made a perfect target. What if something happened to her? No one to see her. No one to hear her. No one to fight for Scotty. The last time she'd felt this vulnerable, she'd been sixteen. Pressure built behind her eyes and her throat worked itself raw.

She almost wished she were back at the estate, letting the Colonel take charge.

Don't talk crazy. Keep moving. Find clothes. Be ready.

She hesitated at the cottage door, knocked, then wrenched the knob. It turned in her hand. The door squealed open, blasting her less-than-moral intentions to break-and-enter to the world.

She wasn't stealing; she was borrowing. She'd give everything back once she'd found Scotty.

Two bunk beds held up the narrow walls of the cabin. Weather-resistant mattresses lined each bunk. One bench crouched beneath the lone window. The smell of must and the bite of wood smoke lingered in the air. No clothes. No boots. Nothing of use at all.

Maybe the next one would prove more fruitful.

Nora made her way to each of the cottages in turn, finding each as empty as the first. An overwhelming sense of powerlessness knocked her to her knees. Head in her hands, the edge of despair threatened to turn her into a sobbing mess. She sniffed back at the thrust of tears. If she started, she wouldn't be able to stop.

Images of Scotty spun a tornado of memories that tormented her. What if they were all she had left of her son?

No! I refuse! She reared back with a roar. She would not collapse. She would stay strong. Scotty was counting on her, and she wouldn't let him down.

Hiking clothes didn't matter. Her cashmere sweater was warm, especially when moving around. The good wool of her slacks was as tough as any material. And her fashion boots sported soles made to grip the sidewalk. She'd handle an afternoon out in the woods just fine. The important thing was to find Scotty before the Colonel did—before dark.

As she scrambled to her feet, the crunching of tires on gravel echoed from the bottom of the drive. Sabriel. Her heart lightened, and she raced down the path, back toward the lodge.

She was about to burst out of the tree-lined trail when she spotted the black Hummer creeping up the drive. Instinct shot her down to a crouch. Three men scuttled out of the vehicle like beetles. Boggs, all six feet of intimidation and testosterone, and two more of the Colonel's muscle with their close-cropped hair, black battle-dress uniforms and black jungle boots.

Impossible. How had they found her?

The sink of letdown knocked her off balance. She grabbed a pine bough and steadied her stance.

Sabriel. He'd betrayed her. Led her like some Marie Antoinette to the guillotine—right where the Colonel could make her head, her whole body disappear.

Voices came at her, bouncing around the woods as if she were surrounded on all sides by a radio not quite tuned in. An angry whisper. A tinny mumble. A conversation where the words made no sense, but sent crawls of warning shivering down her spine.

The blue jays stopped jabbering. The trees no longer swayed. Even the waves on the water lapped at the rocks on the shore in near silence. She couldn't let the thugs corner her. Not until she'd found Scotty.

The Hummer's cooling engine pinged, giving her a start. She scrunched down farther, then inched backward, away from the Colonel's men.

A hand, big and rough, clamped over her mouth. A steel-strapped arm banded across her chest and dragged her backward. A scream tore from her throat, but the vise of a hand securing her mouth muffled it. She fought, twisting and kicking, and worked to free her lips to bite the offending fingers. But the body clinched tight against hers had no give and the flesh might as well have been granite. Her left hip bruised against the hard outline of a holster. Her peripheral vision caught a blur of black and panic ran rampant.

Another of the Colonel's thugs.

She wanted to run. She wanted to scream. But her body was ice, and her breath was gone. The thug said something, but through the thunder of her blood, she couldn't make out the words.

No, let me go. I can't go back to the Colonel's. Not until I find Scotty.

"Shh. It's me. Sabriel." The hiss of his breath rasped hot and urgent in her ear.

Sabriel, who was no savior, but one of *them*. She

wasn't going back. Not without Scotty. Her limbs thawed enough for her to renew her struggle.

"Stop. They'll hear you."

As if he cared. He'd told them where to find her.

He hauled her off her feet as if she weighed no more than a loaf of bread and dragged her deeper into the woods, where he crouched, folding down her uncooperative body along with his. A surge of adrenaline shivered through her. How could she have been so trusting? Just because he was Tommy's friend? Given Tommy's mental state, common sense would have warranted more caution.

"If I take my hand off, will you keep quiet?" Sabriel said in a sandpaper-harsh whisper.

Breathing fast and shallow, she nodded. She needed to save her strength for escape. Give herself time to think. She had to find real help and fast. Where could she go? Not the local police—they were bought and paid for by the Colonel. The resort where Tommy worked? It was far enough from Camden to not give a damn about Camden money. Someone there would help her. Time, all that time, trickling away from her, and Scotty out there, needing her.

Sabriel loosened his hand from her mouth, but continued to press on her shoulders to hold her down. She cranked her head over her left shoulder and caught a glimpse of him. He looked even more dark and dangerous than she remembered with that wild animal caution in those panther-green eyes, that dusky skin and that camouflage gear, fitting into the forest as if he belonged.

Once a Ranger, always a Ranger. Once a Camden soldier, always a Camden soldier?

"You led them to me." Nora's voice cracked. "You're supposed to be Tommy's friend."

"Your car is equipped with a GPS."

That neat little blue button that summoned help with the press of a fingertip. Her shoulders deflated in a sag of surrender. "Of course. Bugged. Just like the phone and the computer." And she'd used her phone repeatedly. Had she left an electronic bread crumb trail for the Colonel's men to follow and not just a record of her calls?

Nora couldn't stop shaking. Even rubbing her arms didn't seem to spawn any heat. The Colonel's men would fan their search in this direction any second. She'd lose Scotty. "I can't let them take me back."

"Then let's roll." Sabriel's gaze scanned forward and back. "Now."

"SHE CAN'T BE FAR." Boggs's craggy voice ping-ponged from tree to tree. "Her engine's still warm. Spread out and find her."

Sabriel allowed his vision to widen, seeking possible danger in the escape route he'd picked. He jerked his head in the direction where he'd left his Jeep, signaling his intent to Nora. Brown eyes dark and wild with fear, she glanced in the goons' direction before following him like a scared mouse.

He was a pushover for women with vulnerable eyes. Always trying to save them when he couldn't save himself. And hers were especially compelling, sucking him in like the most gullible of marks. But he couldn't let her get to him. She was a Camden, and he'd had enough Camden anguish to last him a lifetime.

He'd known from the second his phone rang that it meant trouble, and Nora Camden was proving him right. *Fences, man. You've got to learn to keep up your fences.*

She wouldn't last an hour out in the mountains, especially bushwhacking. Even if it cost him time, he'd get her to the Aerie, where the Colonel and his goons couldn't hurt her.

This time, he'd do things right.

The Colonel's men scattered like cockroaches, not bothering to cushion their steps. Twigs snapped. Leaves rustled like snakes. They didn't care if Nora knew they were coming. They probably wanted her scared. Made the sport more fun. *Pinheads.*

Despite her slight body, Nora wasn't exactly Miss Light Foot as she trailed him, so all the hired guns' noise gave her some cover. But then why should she know how to stalk? A refined woman like her belonged at country clubs and charity balls, surrounded and protected by friends and family. Not running for her life from the megalomaniac who was supposed to keep her safe. He remembered her bright smile, how she'd made Tommy so happy on their wedding day, and wished he'd warned her about the Colonel all those years ago.

Sabriel headed downslope, toward the private road farther west where he'd camouflaged his Jeep. Nora huffed and puffed behind him, but scared to death as she was, she kept pace like a trooper.

The intent footsteps on both sides grew nearer. Two pairs, parallel.

"Here, Nora, Nora, Nora!" the goon on the left taunted—as if she were a dog. Laughter exploded through each syllable at his own little joke.

Sabriel grabbed Nora's arm, making himself a wall between her and the threat. He assessed his position on the fly. Hell. They wouldn't get back to his Jeep fast enough. He had to find some place to hunker down till the goons moved on.

He propelled them toward a rock formation jutting out from the side of a hill up ahead, and hoped, despite the piled scat and acorn shells, that no creature was renting space there at the moment. The last thing he needed was for Nora to scream and give away their location while they were cornered.

Without ceremony, he pushed her into the crevice between two slabs of granite. The space was barely big enough for one, let alone two, but he wedged in front of her, his camo gear blocking out the white flag of her cream sweater. He unsnapped his holster and forced his pulse to slow.

"Don't talk. Don't move. Don't breathe," he whispered into her ear.

Her head rubbed a nervous "okay" against his arm, and the almost forgotten softness of a woman shot static into his muscles and scrambled his thought process for a second. He shoved the thought aside and sought to separate the sounds of the forest from those of the enemy.

In the darkness of the narrow cave, his senses sharpened. But like a compass needle seeking north, they kept bouncing back too close to home.

The sweet almond of her scent, the keenness of her fear, the mossy tang of the earth tugged at memories. Anna and Ranger school. The pills and Tommy. The sweat and the survival. His jaw ground down the unwanted flashes, and he forced his awareness back to his surroundings.

The cool hardness of the rock pressed against his sides. The warmth of the body pinned against his front. Her curves fitting into his knees, hips and shoulders like water. How long had it been since he'd held a woman this close?

Footsteps approached from above, getting nearer, their vibrations pulsing through the soft earth. A distinct crunch and pop that came from no woodland creature broke two feet from their hole. The hitch of Nora's breath against his neck, its intimacy, brought on an unexpected reaction. Hell. He didn't need a complication like that now. He gritted his teeth, squeezing as much space between their bodies as he dared. He needed his senses clear and alert, not jumbled by primitive urges.

She was shaking so hard, he feared the clacking of her bones would attract the hunter's attention. In the cramped space, Sabriel slowly slid his right hand up her arm and cupped it around her nape, releasing calming energy into her body the way Grandma Fiona had taught him, quieting them both.

The roof of moss dipped under a boot, cascading a small avalanche of dirt onto their heads.

The pulse in Sabriel's left hand pounded against the Beretta's cold steel. One man. He could take him. But killing had never come easy, and his life wasn't yet in jeopardy.

The moss ripped. A boot plunged through the opening. The tip of the toe scraped against Sabriel's temple.

Nora's feet climbed his leg like a tree. Her shaking fingers dug into his neck, cutting off his circulation. Her chest beat like a machine gun against his. But somehow she kept her terrified sobs caged.

Something scurried across his boots. Sabriel caught a flash of gray waddling into the clearing, snorting and snuffing.

Thank you, brother porcupine.

"Stop!" the Colonel's man ordered. He rescued his foot from the hole and drew his weapon.

"Got something, Hutt?"

Boggs. Off to the right. Within line of sight.

Don't move, Nora. Whatever you do, don't move. As if she'd heard him, her body went death-still.

"Nothing." Hutt swore. "Just some freaking porcupine."

"Frisk him. He might know something."

"You're a riot, Boggs."

"Keep looking."

"We've already disabled her car. Let's just leave her and come back after we find the kid."

"We don't know who she might have met here. I don't like to leave loose ends behind."

Nora's throat pistoned against Sabriel's shoulder.

Shh. It's okay. I'll get you out of here.

The footsteps faded and disappeared. Sabriel didn't move. He kept listening to the sounds of the woods, much too aware of the woman wrapped around him like a second skin, imprinting herself into his flesh.

Five minutes. Ten.

Only when the high-pitched *chip-chip-chip* of a chipmunk resounded nearby and the watery *toolool* of a blue jay rolled above did Sabriel relax. "They're gone."

"How do you know?" A hint of cinnamon rode on her breath, and he wanted to taste her.

"The birds."

Her breath whooshed in a gust. "They're singing again."

He eased out of the rocky fissure, surveyed the woods, then offered her a hand, which she ignored. She slapped at the dirt sprinkled on the shoulder of her sweater, making the stingy strings of sunlight poking through the trees weave through her brown hair in golden ribbons. "What if they come back?"

"We make sure we're not here." Sabriel cupped her elbow, aware of her delicate bones, of her heat, of her fear, and turned her toward the trail. With Boggs in the mix, finding Tommy was going to be hard enough. He didn't need this extra liability.

As he walked, he reached for his phone and placed a call to Falconer's private number. When Falconer answered, the wedding reception boomed in the background. "Everything okay?"

Sabriel's jaw tensed, and the words ground out with

more bitterness and resentment than he'd intended. "I need help."

He gave Falconer a synopsis of his afternoon.

"I'll alert Kingsley to fire up the computer," Falconer said. "Liv'll have a room waiting for your friend."

Sabriel had no choice but to open what he thought of as a closed chapter in his life to Falconer. He couldn't leave Nora in harm's way. He knew the wrath an angry Thomas Camden could wreak. The goons' guns weren't there simply to prove their manhood. Their orders were to hurt her.

He crushed his eyes closed against the piercing pain of the video he'd watched so often he knew every frame by heart—the drooping hair, the limp body, the bloody foam.

His conscience couldn't stand another death.

Chapter Four

Nora scrunched down in the Jeep's seat, spine rounded, legs pressed together, arms tight against her sides, keeping still and quiet. She'd spent a great deal of her childhood quivering in fear, making herself invisible, yet fear had taken on a new dimension when she'd delivered Scotty and known unconditional love for the first time.

The thought of being pregnant, a mother, had petrified her. She wasn't ready. Tommy wasn't ready. Things were too unstable with the resurgence of his illness and their uncertain future. Then, when the nurse had laid this innocent little creature into her arms, all she'd wanted to do was to knit him back into the protective cocoon of her womb, away from this harsh world's dangers.

She'd tried to protect him, whipping toy trucks and Lego pieces from under his dimpled feet, distracting him from the greenhouse of tempting plants with which his grandmother decorated every room, shielding him from the Colonel's unreasonable expectations.

Love that fervent didn't make you brave, she'd learned, it made you afraid—of everything. And the thought of losing her son—the best part of her—now terrified her like nothing before.

Her only job had been to keep her little boy safe. A job she'd done with a fierceness that bordered on obsession. He would have a happy childhood, if that was the only thing she accomplished.

Overcompensation, she knew. For all the good it had done.

Where was he? Was he warm enough? Was he hungry? Was he breathing?

What would happen to him if the Colonel's men followed their orders and she met with a convenient accident?

On the verge of tears again, she turned to the window. She frowned as a road sign zoomed by. "Shouldn't we be heading north, not south?"

"I'm taking you to a safe house."

She strained against the seat belt. "No! That's not going to work. I can't abandon my son when he needs me."

"I'll find him."

"His medicine—"

"I'll get it to him."

"Do you know *anything* about kids?"

"I'll bring him back." Sabriel's iron hand squeezed hers. "Safe. I promise."

The rigid lines of his face, telling their own tale, negated any reassurance she might have gained from the warm gesture. "Like you did Tommy during Ranger School?"

His hand shot off hers, stinging her with ripped-flesh rawness, and gripped the steering wheel as if he needed its steadying balance.

"I'm sorry. That was out of line." Her cutting comment had hit a still-fresh scar, and she wanted to smooth the hurt. She'd been on the receiving end of cruel words often enough to know better. But her worry for Scotty trumped all and brought out a ruthless streak.

She reached toward Sabriel, but his aura vibrated with an electric-fence intensity that would fry her if she dared to cross its boundary. She folded her hands into her lap. "You're trying to help me. And I'm being ungrateful."

As the Colonel never ceased to remind her whenever she defied any of his orders. And like the Colonel, Sabriel was taking over without asking, expecting her to fall meekly in line and obey.

The worst part was that letting him take over would be easy—too easy. Her spine curved in as if it had lost its anchoring guy wire. She needed his help. He was fit and strong and knew his way around the mountains. He knew how to find Tommy. He knew how to bring Scotty back to her.

Something she could not do for herself.

She flattened her palms on her thighs, shoring up her resolve. She couldn't let fear rule. Not this time. And she couldn't continue to let other people make decisions for her. Especially not when it came to Scotty. Maybe if she'd taken a stronger stand against the Colonel's intrusive meddling, then Tommy wouldn't have felt he had to take Scotty.

"The Aerie's a safe bunker," Sabriel said.

"The Colonel—"

"Won't be able to get to you."

"I'm tougher than I look." Her chin flagged up. "I won't complain. I promise."

"You'll slow me down."

The Jeep bumped over a dip in the road, forcing her to grab onto the dashboard. "I'll keep up. I swear."

"You'll muddle the tracks."

"I'll stay out of your way."

"The best thing you can do for your son is to let me find him. Alone."

He spoke to her as if she were a kindergartner who was having trouble learning how to tie her shoes. Her back stiffened. "Do you know anything about asthma? What if Tommy can't cope? Can you handle him when he's in a manic phase? Or, even worse, when he's scraping the bottom of the depression barrel?"

"No one can reach him then."

"I can talk Tommy down. I can talk him up. I've done it before." Like in that first year when the Colonel had forced Tommy to move back to the estate and sent Tommy's mental balance in a tailspin. "I know how to handle Scotty's asthma. When to keep pushing the drugs, when to ease back."

"You said yourself that Tommy trusts me."

"Thing is that Tommy can't be trusted—not if he's off his meds. What if he's tackled a situation that's too big for him and he's hurt? How are you going to carry both Tommy and Scotty off those mountains?"

"I'll call for a rescue."

"And how long would that take?" She wanted to slap him up the side of the head. "We've already wasted too much time." Why couldn't he see that?

"This isn't going to be a walk in the park." Sabriel spoke in measured beats, but ripples of emotions still swelled beneath the glass-smooth surface of his voice. "We're talking about a killer pace over rough terrain and steep grades. There are no flush toilets out there. No maids to cook your meals or turn down your bed. When was the last time you walked uphill for more than ten minutes?"

She glared at him, the heat of battle rising up her neck, burning her cheeks. "What do you think I am? A spoiled debutante?"

"I think you're unprepared for the hardships you're going to find out there."

How could she be putting all of her hopes of finding Scotty in this man when he couldn't grasp a simple concept? He saw her as a pampered socialite, but he didn't know she'd already hit bottom once, what she'd done to climb back out of that hole. But even all of that was nothing compared to what she was willing to endure for her son. "To find Scotty, I'd go to hell and back."

He turned to stare at her and his eyes churned in a jungle storm of thunder and lightning that made her want to both reach for him and shrink away. "Do you think those goons tracking you are just playing at soldier?"

I don't like to leave loose ends behind, Boggs had said.

She jutted her chin. "Would you rather they get ahead? That they find Tommy first?"

Sabriel's gaze snapped back to the road and his jaw ground a tight circle. "You have no idea what you're asking."

Guilt. God, she'd wallowed in that tapioca-pudding feeling enough to recognize its lumpy texture. Was it because of Anna? He hadn't been there when she'd died in a freediving accident. Did he feel he was somehow to blame?

It's okay, she wanted to say. *I understand. I've been there.* But he would think she was weak, and he needed to think of her as strong.

"When was the last time you saw Tommy?" Nora asked. "Ten, eleven years ago?" She didn't give him a chance to answer. "You have no idea what kind of mess you're walking in to. Tommy can't control one of Scotty's asthma attacks. He'll panic. Scotty could die."

"Ah, hell," Sabriel said, as if his bad day had suddenly gotten worse. His gaze worked the mirrors and his demeanor braced for impending attack.

Nora sat up and scoured the blurring landscape outside the Jeep. "What's wrong?"

"The Colonel's men."

No! Not now. Not when she was so close to reaching those mountains and saving Scotty. She whipped to look behind them. "I don't see anything."

The black Hummer crested a hill and roared up on them with surprising speed, dust mushrooming around it like an atomic cloud.

An arm popped out of the passenger's window.

A shot ripped out, shattering her mirror. She yelped. Sabriel rammed her head into her lap. "Stay down."

A bullet smashed through the rear window and blew out the front windshield where her head had been only moments ago. *No, no, no, no, no.* The denial ricocheted around her skull. This wasn't part of the plan. No loose end. *Nonononono.* "They're going to kill us."

"Hang tight."

Sabriel yanked on the parking brake and twisted the steering wheel. The Jeep spun.

"Noooooo! Are you crazy?" she sputtered. "I can't die. Scotty—" The rest of her thought splintered in the reckless reel, whirling the world around.

Sabriel released the brake and sped up. Breathless, she tried to sit up. He shoved her head down again, but not before she caught a glimpse of the speedometer. Sixty. On a twisting, hilly dirt road. They were going to die. Bullets or a crash. Either way the outcome would leave her dead and Scotty at the Colonel's mercy.

"Hold on," Sabriel said.

To what? Her sanity? He was shredding that faster than a cat could a brand-new chair arm.

She screamed at the unexpected impact of Hummer grille against Jeep fender. The clash sent a shock wave reverberating all the way into her bones. Glass shattered. Metal crumpled. The *whump* of a bullet pelted the bumper. Another thwacked into the glove compartment, springing it open, dumping its contents on her head.

This wasn't the way she'd planned to die. It was

supposed to happen when she was old and tired. In her sleep. Not compacted between two trucks. Not made into a sieve by bullets. Her hands tightened around her ankles and her shaking knees bumped into her nose.

Sabriel kept on speeding. She couldn't see what was happening outside the Jeep, couldn't anticipate his moves. *He knows what he's doing.* She swallowed hard. *He's a trained soldier, a trained agent. He'll keep you safe.*

The sudden sharp turn caught her unprepared, throwing her sideways against his hard thigh like a rag doll, then smacked her back against the door.

"Are you all right?" he asked as he hurled the Jeep along a maze of twisty, tree-lined back roads.

"Just peachy."

"Are you hit?"

She scanned through the cotton numbness of her limbs and shook her head.

"You can sit up."

She wasn't sure she could. Her fingers wouldn't unclamp from her ankles and her spine didn't seem to have any starch. She was cold, so cold, as if ice water flowed through her veins and chilled her from the inside out. *Normal. It's been a crazy day.* Tommy taking Scotty. Lying to the Colonel. Being shot at. Her voice croaked up her throat. "We lost them?"

"For now."

Her body finally cooperated and she sat up. She rubbed her arms and could not get a kilocalorie of warmth into her body. "Scotty. We can't let them get to Scotty."

"I won't."

On the main road up ahead, sirens shrieked in the dying afternoon. Blue lights swirled through the bleeding sky in a mottled tapestry of bruises. Nora swiveled her head to look over her shoulder. The Hummer wasn't in sight. But it was back there, somewhere in that ant's nest of dirt roads, hunting for them.

They were trapped.

And they were still in Camden country. The two police cruisers blocking the road were not there to help them.

A loose end.

Forward or back would lead them straight into the Colonel's clutches.

He would once again get what he wanted—her out of the picture and Scotty to himself.

I'm sorry, baby, so sorry.

Sabriel swore and steered the Jeep into the trees. Nora hung on to the dashboard as they catapulted onto a barely-there rut.

In spite of her tight grip, the ride bobbed her like a cork in a fast-moving stream. And like that cork, she had no control over her situation.

"Tree!" she squealed as Sabriel almost hit an oak.

"I see it."

"Could you slow down?"

She might as well have spit into the wind for all the good her request did. He kept racing ahead, the sharp cranking of the steering wheel jostling her from side to side.

"If we crash," she said, "they get what they want. Us dead."

"You want the cops to hold us until it's too late to find Tommy?"

"I want to get to the damn mountains and find my son. Preferably alive."

Sabriel made a bone-rattling entry into a snarl of bushes and braked to a jarring halt, killing the engine.

A minute later, the black Hummer crept by on the narrow track they'd left. Sabriel remained unfazed, a statue in his seat, while she turned into a quivering mass of ringing nerves.

How could he stay so calm when everything was falling apart? They could end up dead before they ever reached the mountains and Scotty.

"The Colonel's men tried to kill us," she said, watching the taillights, red evil eyes, retreat into the darkening woods.

"The Colonel wants his grandson," Sabriel said. "And what the Colonel wants, the Colonel goes after."

"No matter who gets hurt."

Sabriel's jaw flinched. "Collateral damage."

Nora rubbed at the tightness in her throat with one ice-cold hand. "He wants to control Scotty like he controlled Tommy and Anna. And look how that turned out." Her gaze speared Sabriel's jungle-green eyes. "I can't let that happen."

In the depth of his steady gaze, she found reassurance. An understanding that went soul deep. For the first time in her life, someone was seeing her. Really seeing her, and not flinching at what he saw there. He knew. He understood. The Colonel had almost broken him, too. But he'd survived, and that gave her hope. Heat returned to her cold limbs, and she wanted to linger there in the calming balm of his sight.

Sabriel broke the odd connection pulsing between them and studied the woods until the Hummer was out of range. "We'll find your son."

She took his promise to heart.

He cranked over the engine and continued his mapless track through the woods.

"I can't guarantee your safety out on the trail," he said.

"Safety means nothing to me as long as Scotty's out there."

A few minutes later, without so much as a touch of the brakes, Sabriel shot out onto a two-lane road. At least it was asphalt and relatively smooth. Her tentacle grip on the dashboard loosened.

Sabriel whipped on the headlights, shifted gears and sped up. He was heading north. Relief fluxed through her muscles. She didn't want to fight him, but she would if it meant saving Scotty.

The day faded to night, leaving behind a black so deep the headlights barely cut through its thickness. Sabriel's profile slashed a jagged silhouette in the dim glow of the instrument panel. High cheekbones. A nose like an Indian brave's in a Beverly Doolittle print. Square chin. The yellow cast of the light burnished his skin to dark copper. A good face. A strong face. One that wouldn't crumple under the Colonel's will.

Afraid Sabriel would change his mind and turn the

Jeep south again, Nora sat flagpole straight, hands folded in her lap, gaze on the road.

The silence between them grew until it was as dense as the darkness around them.

Her fingers itched to crank the radio full blast, tune in to a rock station, blow the roof right off the Jeep. She needed drums. Big, banging drums. Lots of drums. Entrain—"Rise Up," "River Run," "Mo Drums." Loud enough to drown out the beat of her doubts driving her crazy.

She was at his mercy, just as she'd been at the Colonel's and at her mother's. And look where that had landed her. A wuss afraid of her own shadow, begging for just another chance.

I'll be good, Mommy, please, I promise. Just don't leave.

I'll accept your terms, Colonel. Please, just don't take my baby away from me.

I won't complain. I promise, Sabriel. Please, just help me find my son.

"TELL ME ABOUT Tommy," Sabriel said.

Though he appeared to study the road, Nora was acutely aware that he was watching her. For signs of a meltdown? *Won't happen.* Not until she found Scotty. "Like what?"

"His mental state."

Tommy with his mischievous smile, his eclectic playlists and his unabashed shows of affection. At eighteen, starving as she'd been for attention, she'd fallen for his easy charm. So fast. Too fast. She'd never suspected that pharmaceuticals were holding him together. Not until it was too late. Regret rolled around her heavy heart.

"He seemed to be doing so well. He'd finally found a psychiatrist that got him." She snorted. "One that wouldn't report back to the Colonel."

"What about his meds?"

"What about them?" A certain protectiveness where Tommy was concerned brought up caution.

"You said you thought he was off his meds."

She'd forgotten the desperation of her pleas. "I thought he was keeping up." She picked at the pale pink polish on her thumbnail. Had she missed the signs? The few minutes of conversation they shared when Tommy picked up Scotty weren't enough to pass judgment. Not with the Colonel standing guard more often than not, listening to their exchange.

But in the past few months, Tommy had turned back to the man she'd fallen in love with eleven years ago. Sweet, funny, loving. But that was the danger point, wasn't it? When the patient thought he was well enough to do without the meds. She shrugged and shook her head. "Taking Scotty like this, though…I don't know."

"Do you know the name of his psychiatrist?"

"You won't get anything from him. Patient-doctor confidentiality."

"Kingsley can."

"Kingsley?"

"Seekers' computer expert."

She didn't dare ask how, just savored the relief that

someone could tell her if Tommy was a threat to Scotty. *Sorry, Tommy. It's for your own good, for Scotty's.* "Dr. Montgomery at the Whiteside Clinic."

"What was Scotty wearing when he left?"

What had she noticed missing in his room? Was it only this morning? It felt more like a week.

"His clothing could snag against branches," Sabriel offered before she could answer—as if he was trying to make up for his earlier brusqueness, but didn't quite know how to go about it. "Could let me know where he's been."

Nora nodded and knitted her fingers into her lap. "Red backpack. Yellow fleece jacket. Camouflage pants. Hiking boots."

"What else?"

"I didn't exactly have time to take inventory."

"A backpack's a good sign." The words hitched out as if acts of comfort were foreign to him. "Tommy probably had him pack layers."

If Scotty had layers, then he'd stay warm at night and maybe his asthma wouldn't flare up. The hopeful thought soothed the raw edge of her nerves.

"Tell me about his footwear."

"Why?" One of her heels clacked against the floor mat like a manic drummer hammering the pedal of a bass drum and Nora wished she could get up and move instead of being strapped in this car seat doing nothing.

"So I know what kind of tracks to look for." Sabriel's voice remained smooth and even, but she sensed the calmness cost him.

She'd promised herself she wouldn't be a burden to

him, so she dug deep. Try as she might, she couldn't picture the boots. "Tommy got Scotty hiking boots for his birthday last September. He gets a discount at work. I don't know the brand. Brown. That's all I remember."

"Size?"

A small yelp escaped her. "That, I know. Size six."

"Hiking poles?"

She didn't think Scotty had any, but that didn't mean Tommy hadn't provided him with some. "I don't know."

"What time did they leave? Your best guess."

Her head ached and her thoughts snarled in a mess. To keep from falling apart, she went back to scratching the pink polish off her nails. "Scotty went to bed at eight. I checked on him at ten. I let him sleep in this morning because he'd had several asthma attacks over the week, and he needed extra sleep. If I'd checked in on him when I got up—"

"They could still have had hours of lead time."

On a logical level, she understood this, but emotionally, she kept thinking that she could have done something more. That, if she'd only been more observant, she could have prevented this nightmare.

Sabriel tapped his thumbs against the steering wheel, reeling her back to the present. "What kind of outdoor experience does Scotty have?"

Scotty talked about the hikes he and his father took on their Saturdays together. But two hours every other weekend wasn't very long and kept them close to home.

"He's hiked with Tommy since he was little," Nora said, but the true answer was another *I don't know.*

How could she know so little about her own son? The one person she spent most of her days with? The one person she thought she knew better than herself?

"His asthma keeps him from most sports." Much to the Colonel's irritation. "Especially in the winter when the cold triggers attacks." Cold like tonight. And last night. Was he okay?

"Other than the asthma, is he in good health?"

Sabriel's question derailed her grim train of thought once again. And she finally understood that the interrogation was in part meant to keep her from drowning in worry. Why in the world was that clinical approach so comforting? *Because you're a mess, Nora.* She had to stay strong, and his calm questions were keeping her afloat, giving her a steady anchor. "Just the normal scrapes and bruises."

"What about injuries?"

She frowned. "What do you mean?"

"Has he ever broken a leg or an arm?"

"Why would that make the difference?"

"Could alter his tracks."

Oh. "Nothing."

Sabriel knew how to look, what to look for. They would find Scotty. She knew it. "After a day? How hard will it be to pick up their trail?"

"If it doesn't rain, the tracks should hold."

She looked outside at the stygian night, so dark, so cold. No moon. No stars. That meant clouds. And clouds could mean rain. Her tongue turned to cotton and sweat prickled her armpits. How could she be sweating and yet feel so cold?

"What kind of kid is Scotty?" Sabriel asked.

There he was again, saving her from her dire thoughts with his question and part of her turmoil quieted. "He's a great kid. Sweet, smart. Smarter than the Colonel gives him credit for."

"What does he look like?"

"He's small for his age." Which somehow seemed like a failure on her part when the Colonel looked at her son with disappointment in his eyes. "He has Tommy's wild blond curls." Blond curls he twirled around a finger when he slept—just as he'd done with her hair while he'd nursed. "Brown eyes like mine." They sparkled when he recounted his adventures with his father.

She couldn't help the small smile that formed at the familiar tug on her heart when she thought about her son. "Only one of his cheeks dimples when he smiles. His feet look too big for his small body, and he bounces in place when he's excited and can't contain himself." *Not helpful, Nora.*

She pressed her temple against the cool window glass and noticed that Sabriel listened to her babble with studious intent, as if what she left out was as important as what she said.

At her pause, he glanced in her direction. "Go on."

But she didn't want to lean on him too much, to lose herself again because it was easier not to rock the boat than to swim on her own. "Didn't Tommy ever send you pictures?"

Sabriel gave a quick shake of his head. "What about hobbies and interests?"

"What happened between the two of you?"

The tendons along Sabriel's jaw became taut wires. "Hobbies?"

"Tommy says you're the only person he can trust, yet you two never talk."

"Not related to the situation."

"What if it is?"

"Hobbies?" Sabriel insisted with a quiet, yet unmistakable authority.

"You're asking me to pour my guts out, but you can't give me a single speck of something in return?"

His jaw slid from side to side. "You came to me for my skill, not my history."

"But they're related. By the Colonel."

"Because of the Colonel, I'll help Tommy."

Cringing at the sting of his words, Nora went back to peeling away the pink nail polish. Still, something had happened to turn a treasured friendship into a net of guilt and regret. What had happened at Ranger School? Was there more? Was it because of Anna? Nora shook the thoughts of Tommy and Anna and Sabriel and their complicated relationship out of her mind. She had to concentrate on Scotty. He was her priority—finding him, getting him home safely was all that mattered.

"Scotty loves to read," she said, hoping to defuse the tension she'd caused. She still needed Sabriel's help. "Which the Colonel doesn't consider a manly endeavor." She snorted. "As if generals were born knowing everything there was to know about strategy without ever cracking open a book."

A montage of Scotty moments flashed into her memory like a photo album and not thinking about all the blank pages she'd hoped to fill in the years to come took all of her effort. "Everything about the outdoors interests him. Plants. Animals. Bugs."

"Like Tommy."

She nodded.

"Right- or left-handed?"

"Left. Like Tommy. Why?" She turned in her seat to take a better look at the man who knew so much about the man who'd fathered her child, about how to find him and rescue her son. She gave a prayer of thanks that Tommy had such a loyal friend.

"Right-handed people tend to circle to the right," Sabriel said.

The unfinished thought implied left-handed people would tend to circle left.

"A trail is a string of clues," Sabriel said. "The more I know, the faster I can follow."

Without signaling, he turned into the trees. She gasped and grabbed the dashboard, bracing for a collision. Were the Colonel's men back? Her glance zipped to the missing mirror and met nothing but darkness.

The seat belt jammed into her chest, stealing her breath, but the Jeep kept moving forward—not directly into the trees, but down a narrow lane.

The Jeep bounced along the rutted dirt track barely wide enough for the tires. Tree branches, bushes and weeds scratched along the sides and the undercarriage of the truck in a nails-on-chalkboard grate.

How far had they gone? Far enough to have found Tommy's starting point? The black landscape gave away none of its secrets.

"Where are we?" she asked as her breath returned.

Sabriel stopped before a primitive gate of weathered planks. A red stop sign, whose phosphorescent paint flared in the headlights' beams, warned, "Private Property. Keep Out. Trespassers Will Be Shot."

Sabriel said, "Welcome to your corner of hell."

Chapter Five

The Jeep's headlights sliced across a clearing where a ramshackle cabin squatted. The building stooped old-man crooked with its sagging tin roof spine, liver spots of mold and cracked board skin.

A string of questions lashed at Nora's mind, but she didn't voice any of them. She let them turn inside her mouth until their knots lost their sharp flavor. But the words *Can I trust you?* kept buzzing in her ear with a bloodthirsty mosquito whine. Was this just another ploy to strand her while Sabriel charged into the wilds alone?

What choice did she have other than to trust him? Going back to the Colonel? Losing Scotty?

Not a chance.

Sabriel powered the Jeep right up to the front steps, then rummaged in the backseat and emerged with a headlamp.

"Why are we stopping?" Nora asked, frantic to keep going.

"Supplies."

Supplies made sense. They couldn't go trekking

through the mountains without food or water. But the place looked as if no one had set foot there in decades. "Here?"

He didn't answer, but unlocked the padlock guarding the door and disappeared inside, leaving her alone in the dark. A restless edge nagged at her that they were wasting time. Each minute they stopped allowed Tommy to take Scotty farther away from her, gave the Colonel another chance to find her son before she could.

Help him. It'll go faster.

She scrambled out of the Jeep. The damp scent of night and decaying leaves pressed against her as she headed to the cabin. The wind's cold fingers chased her inside.

Groping the darkness, Nora stepped into the scrubby building. She'd never seen a dark so deep. In the city, there were always lights. At the Colonel's, the security spotlights turned midnight into midday. Here nothing, except for the tiny beam attached to Sabriel's head. Going suddenly blind must feel like this.

How was Scotty handling this black hole of night? Surely, Tommy had thought to bring along flashlights.

Sabriel's light bounced crazily against the cracked wood of the walls, highlighting snakes of cobwebs, fangs of trusses and skeletons of cupboards.

Nora followed Sabriel to the back of the building. "Is this your place?"

He grunted and stopped.

She bumped into his hard body and rebounded just as quickly, but had to grasp his forearm for balance. The subtle scent of mint and pine struck her now as it had when they'd hidden in the fissure of rock at the adventure camp. Clean. Pleasant. Masculine. Heat rose to her face. Hanging on to him like that wasn't the way to prove she could stay on her own two feet, that she wouldn't get in his way. "Don't you have electricity?"

"I'll get the oil lamp in a bit."

Sabriel crouched before a metal trunk the color of dried blood under the focused beam of his headlamp. His hands gripped the decorative brass corners with a ferocity that turned his knuckles white. He closed his eyes and bent his head forward as if in prayer.

His hands shot across the lid, then hesitated above the brass clasp. With an explosion of breath that sounded as if someone was peeling his skin, he ripped the clasp open and threw back the cover. The crack was like a seal breaking, releasing the scent of cedar into the air. He pawed through the contents, though she could swear he saw nothing, then shoved pants, fleece and long underwear at her.

"These should fit." He shut the lid with a decisive snap. "You look about the same size."

Anna. Nora's throat dammed. He was giving her Anna's things. He'd kept them all this time, and now he was handing over his treasure. Her heart went out to him. She hadn't realized that helping her would force him to rip open so many wounds.

From what Tommy had told her, the Colonel had ruined Sabriel's promising Army career after he'd eloped with Anna. Sabriel had barely survived the Colonel's vengeance. And helping her was pitting him once again against the Colonel. She would have a lot to make up to him once Scotty was safe.

She gave a small nod. "Thank you."

Sabriel grunted and strode toward the front of the cabin.

She trotted after him. "No, I mean it. I appreciate…everything."

"If I'm going to drag you through the mountains, I don't want you holding me back because you're cold and your fancy boots are slipping all over the place."

"You're right." The words rushed out, afraid she'd made another mistake, afraid he'd leave her behind. "I'm sorry."

Sabriel located the oil lamp on the lone shelf flanked by two cupboards. The flame from his lighter sparked the wick to life, throwing the single room into a soft light that erased the sharp corners and wrapped them in a cocoon that felt too intimate.

"Dress in layers," he said, his voice strangely thick, and headed toward the door.

"Where are you going?" A quick march of panic trampled her chest. *Don't leave me alone.*

He slanted her a wry smile. "Want me to stay for the striptease?"

Heat rushed up her neck and pooled in her cheeks. "Uh, no, that's okay."

"I'll go chase the skunks out of the outhouse while you change."

Skunks? He had to be joking. "It's not going to work."

He raised an eyebrow.

"Scaring me. I'm not going back. Not without Scotty."

He shook his head, the tilt of a smile and the gleam of approval quickly hidden as he turned the headlamp back on before heading out. "Tommy always said nothing could scare you."

He had? Wow, she'd put up a really good front then, because everything scared her. More than she'd like to admit. Not even sleep could guarantee her a respite—not with the recurring nightmares chasing her awake, drenched in sweat. In them, she'd find herself alone, cowered in a dark corner, shivering as the sordid sounds of the night echoed in her skull, in her bones, in her blood, waiting, praying, begging for her mother to come back.

But she'd survived. She'd found a way. And for Scotty she would again.

"Tommy's right." Her chin kicked up. "Nothing you can say or do will scare me."

The click of the door closing was her only answer.

She stacked the borrowed clothes on the table and took off her leather boots, wool slacks and cashmere sweater—peeling away the layers of Nora Camden until all that was left was Nora Picard, who had survived the streets of Boston and fought to make a life for herself. Even though she'd lived surrounded by comfort at the Camden estate, part of her could never quite silence the insecurity of her childhood. She didn't want that fate for Scotty.

She wanted this over. She wanted Scotty safe. She wanted her quiet life back—imperfect as it was.

But things could never be the same. She could never let the Colonel have that much control over Scotty—or her—again. She didn't know how she would do it, but she had to take her son away from the prison of the mansion.

Sabriel had survived his attack. She could, too.

The bracing air of this cold October night licked at her bare skin. She reached for Anna's things and thrust into them as if they were armor. The arms and legs were an inch too long, and the top and long johns fit a tad too snugly.

Anna had been tall and wafer-thin—like her mother. Nora had never quite managed to attain the Camden-perfect figure. She liked food too much. Another tick against her in the Colonel's eyes.

Nora slipped on a pair of thick gray socks. She'd never met Anna. Her sister-in-law had died three weeks before Nora had met Tommy. Tommy had admired his sister's strength to turn her back on family expectations and do what she wanted to do, damn the Colonel and the consequences. The Colonel had cut her off without a penny, disowned her, and refused to let any of the family attend her funeral.

She couldn't imagine what it had been like for Sabriel to endure Anna's death alone, shunned by the family that should have supported him in his grief. Even Tommy hadn't had the strength to defy the Colonel to go to his best friend's side or mourn his sister.

Yet Anna was one of the reasons Nora and Tommy had connected so deeply and so fast. Loss had a language of its own, and they'd both understood it.

She zipped up the last layer of fleece and warmth enfolded her for the first time since she'd left the estate. Maybe her sister-in-law's courage would seep into her bones and complement Sabriel's strength to see her through this ordeal.

Hang on, Scotty. I'm coming for you.

SABRIEL STEPPED onto the weed-choked path outside old Will Daigle's shack, glad for a reprieve from Nora. Her stubborn insistence and vulnerability were wearing on him like a fresh blister. Having lived under the Colonel's influence for so long, he hadn't expected her to have so much steel left in her spine.

He let habit navigate him around the perimeter of the clearing so he could give Nora privacy and him a chance to arm the early-warning system the paranoid codger had set up years ago.

He'd racked his brain for a safe place to protect Nora until he could bring her son and Tommy back. No place was safe around here. Not while the Colonel was bent on one of his "missions." Taking her back to the Aerie would eat up too much time. And he couldn't put anyone else in the path of danger.

He glanced at the jagged outline of old Will's shack. It was really nothing more than four walls and a roof that barely offered protection against the elements. Yet the memories of Will and what he'd taught two runaway boys were more precious than the rising real estate values, and neither Sabriel nor Tommy could bear the thought of selling the land Will had left them after he'd died.

Still, coming here was hard. Between Will, Tommy and Anna, memories stuffed every crack of those drafty walls. Breathing room for all of them.

Do not *open that Pandora's box.*

Keeping a watchful eye on the shack, he whipped out his phone and placed a call to Seekers.

Kingsley answered.

"Shouldn't you be out dancing with that pretty blonde I saw you eyeing at the church?" Sabriel asked, putting off the inevitable, hating to drag anyone else into his personal business.

"Yeah, I was just getting ready to put on my big move when some jerk called for intelligence."

Leaning against a tree, Sabriel laughed, taking the jibe in the playful spirit it was meant and gave back in turn. "You know that cool deejay ploy doesn't work."

He imagined Kingsley in his court, as they jokingly called the command center. Computers, monitors and a myriad of electronic gadgetry jammed every inch of desk and wall space, and Kingsley conducted them all like an accomplished maestro.

"Ah," Kingsley said, "but this was a really sick set. She was falling deeper in love with me with every song."

"You've got to get a life, man."

Kingsley snorted. "Like you're one to talk."

"Me, I've been places, done things. You're too young to be a lonely old man spending all your time in basements."

"I'm not lonely."

But the prickly tone told Sabriel he'd hit a nerve. "When was the last time you went out with friends?"

"I have friends." A grunt. "What's with all the concern, anyway? I didn't know you had that many words in you." Kingsley's chair squeaked. "Besides, I was just e-mailing a friend in Seattle before you called."

"Bill Gates?"

The sound of flesh hitting flesh smacked through the line. "Whoa, hold the presses. Mercer told a joke."

"Ha, ha." Sabriel's lips quirked, knowing that the rest of the Seekers saw him as a stone. But his smile fell as a shadow crossed the lone window of the shack. Nora. She'd stacked Anna's clothes on the dusty table and was now peeling the dirt-smudged sweater from her body.

Turn away, he ordered himself. But mesmerized by the play of mellow light on pale skin, he couldn't seem to pry his gaze from the sight. She pulled the neck of the sweater over her head, making his palm itch to skate down the inviting slope of her back. The gold in her hair gleamed like pyrite as it cascaded back down her shoulders. He sucked in a breath at the imagined feel of silk against his skin.

"You okay?" Kingsley asked.

"Fine." Yeah, just great. He was ogling Tommy's wife like a regular Peeping Tom. Ex-wife, he reminded himself. Not that it mattered. She was the one woman on earth he needed to stay away from.

Biting back a curse, he tore his gaze to the night and focused on the information he needed from Kingsley. "Got anything on the Colonel's employees?"

"Yeah, with a little scanning, firewalking and banner grabbing, I was able to get through in five minutes."

Sabriel grunted. "That's so comforting."

Kingsley chuckled. "Isn't it, though?"

"I'm looking specifically for something on Boggs and Hutt."

Computer keys clacked in a toccata. "Two of the dozen ex-Army Camden has working security for him, both at home and at the lab. Melvyn Boggs is head of security. Been there for nine years. An ex-Ranger like you."

They'd gotten their gold and black tabs in the same class, but that didn't mean they were pals. Boggs might be persistent, focused, driven, confident and determined, but as far as Sabriel was concerned, he'd failed the humble, honest and selfless portions of the Ranger doctrine.

"Dane Hutt started two years ago," Kingsley continued. "Ex-infantry. Both have clean records. No arrests. No convictions. Nothing to say they aren't upstanding members of the community. Fits the rest of the team. All angels as far as the law is concerned."

Like all the Colonel's dirty business. "Sanitized?"

Kingsley made a noise that was a cross between annoyance and anticipation. "That's going to require more digging."

Sabriel couldn't help himself. He glanced back at the shack's window. Nora, clad in Anna's fleece jacket, sat on the chair and was pulling on Anna's socks.

He didn't know why he'd kept the clothes. Maybe because the Colonel had made such a big deal about wanting every stitch that had belonged to Anna after her death. She'd last worn them on their honeymoon— almost twelve years ago. A hike in the mountains, just the two of them and all that endless space. Waking up next to her with the sunlight painting the sky pink and purple and the song of nature around them had seemed like heaven.

Then they'd had to get back to the real world, where the Colonel had pushed and pushed and pushed until Anna had cracked.

"Can you tap into medical records?" Sabriel asked, turning his back on the window once more.

"Illegal."

"But not impossible."

Kingsley's sly smile came through in his voice. "There's always a way to formulate need-to-know."

Sabriel hated to breach Tommy's trust, but he needed to know the state of Tommy's mind. "Thomas Prescott Camden the Fourth. I need to know if he's kept up with his medical care for his bipolar disorder." If Tommy was off his meds and delusional, or stone-cold sane. Each would require different tracking tactics.

"Do you know who's treating him?"

"A Dr. Montgomery at the Whiteside Clinic."

He glanced Nora's way again. She sat, hands in her lap, and stared out the window. Though she couldn't see him out here surrounded by darkness, it seemed as if she were looking right at him and, for an instant, she struck him as utterly lost.

He swallowed a growl. She was getting to him, and he couldn't let that happen.

He finished his call to Kingsley and stalked toward the gate and Will's visitor-deterrent contraption.

Nora's helplessness wasn't his fault. Neither was Tommy's illness. Or the situation they'd jammed their son into.

So why did he feel so frigging guilty?

Because he hadn't watched Tommy's back. Because Anna was dead. Because the Colonel had cornered Nora, and there was no way in hell she'd win a showdown against him. The fight wasn't fair—an ant against an elephant. She'd get squashed.

Just like Anna.

His beautiful mermaid who'd chosen her own path and soothed his restless spirit. She'd made him feel— for a little while, anyway—as if he could do anything. But even the peace she'd found freediving couldn't quite unshackle her from the Colonel's soul-stealing noose. In the end, she'd chosen death over life. The Colonel over him.

Nora, with her soft skin and tender heart, wouldn't stand a chance.

A HALF HOUR later, back inside old Will's shack, Sabriel primed the ancient pump bolted to the floor with water from his pack, then hand-cranked it until water flowed clear into the bucket that served as a sink.

The scent of must and neglect thickened the inside air. A woolly blanket of dust covered the makeshift counter, the lone chair and the table. Mazes of spiderwebs hung from the corners and mice had done a good job of shredding the cot mattress to bits. But otherwise the place had held up well, considering.

He filled the Jetboil's bowl with water and let the flame heat it up while he located the freeze-dried meal pouches he'd stowed in the bear bag in his pack.

Looking at Nora hurt.

All shriveled up on the handmade chair like a discarded doll, watching him with her big, brown eyes as if he were a wolf ready to eat her up. He couldn't deny the hunger was there, but hell, he wasn't in the habit of taking what wasn't offered. He wasn't about to start now. Not with her.

"Is this where Tommy started?" Nora asked.

Sabriel wasn't used to having to explain his every move, and he couldn't say why he stubbornly kept his uncertainties about this mission's tactics to himself. "You need food."

"I'm not hungry."

"Food is fuel. I'm not going to carry you."

"I'm a big girl. I can walk on my own."

"We eat. We rest. We plan."

Before she could insist he share those unformed plans, he grabbed the sorry excuse for a broom Will had left behind and, while the hot water rehydrated their dinner, he swept the floor just enough so they wouldn't spend the night sneezing up dust.

Tommy's plan had been simple enough. The note he'd left Nora had told Sabriel Tommy planned on leaving signs with embedded messages—a code they'd perfected as kids. But Tommy had failed to take two things into consideration: Nora's determination and the Colonel's men. Boggs especially would prove a challenge.

Alone, Sabriel could have followed Tommy, erased his signs and left precious little of his own. But with Nora tagging along, he might as well have marked their trail with neon paint. Keeping her safe while tracking and countertracking wasn't going to be an easy task.

She'd shown spine, though, and she had a high motivation factor. She wouldn't quit on him.

Gaze averted from her clothes—Anna's clothes—he handed her a pouch of beef stew and a titanium spork. He wanted to bury his nose into the navy fleece, drink in what little of Anna's scent was left in the folds of the material before it evaporated. But he was smart enough to resist. She wasn't Anna, but she was a Camden, and that could only bring disaster. "Eat."

Without saying a word, she obeyed.

He shoved aside the mice-eaten mattress, sat on the cot's rusty springs and dug into his stew. He had to give her credit. She was staying true to her word. She wasn't complaining.

In the glow of the oil lamp, she looked both wired and exhausted. The spinning of her mind and the race of her pulse tattooed into him like a Morse code SOS, prodding his tension up another notch.

He wanted her to nag, damn it. He wanted to have a reason to dislike her. He didn't want to care. He couldn't afford to let this get personal. But there she was, all porcelain skin and doe eyes, and all he wanted to do was scoop her up and put her under bulletproof glass.

Instead, he speared a chunk of potato from the pouch

and concentrated on chewing. *You're one lucky son of a bitch, Tommy. I wouldn't do this for just anybody.*

Sabriel's appetite vanished, but he forced himself to finish his meal. The mountain had no mercy for weakness.

He cleaned up while she used the outhouse, then handed her a sleeping bag when she returned. "Get some sleep. We're leaving early in the morning."

"What about a plan?"

"I'm working on it."

Her eyes lifted to meet his gaze, the brown irises swirling with panic. "But they'll get ahead."

"Tommy'll have to stop for the boy."

"We could catch up."

He raised an eyebrow. "With you stumbling over your feet in dark and unfamiliar territory?"

"The Colonel's men—"

"Are still looking for the starting point."

She frowned. "How do you know?"

He didn't, but she was too tired to go on. She'd need all her strength for tomorrow's hike. "They're chasing us."

She gulped. "We're safe here?"

He offered her what he hoped was a reassuring smile. "Old Will had a few tricks up his sleeve to keep unwanted visitors out. We'll hear them coming and be gone before they get to us."

"If you're sure." She spread out the sleeping bag on the floor and zipped it up around her. Using the bundled outer layer of fleece as a pillow, she rolled to her side. "It's cold out there."

Sabriel blew out the oil lamp. Half a smile tugged at

one corner of his mouth. Beaten, scared, but still fighting for her son if not for herself. "Scotty'll be fine. Tommy knows these mountains. He'll keep him snug."

She made a sound that fell short of agreement. "I could help you plan."

"I need to think." No need to scare her with his worries about Boggs.

Sabriel rolled out his sleeping bag on the opposite side of the table and climbed in. The ragged pull of her breaths, the restless rustle of fleece on nylon, filled the darkness with a warm intimacy he'd forgotten. He turned toward her, arms aching at the memory she stirred of Anna.

He missed her. Missed sleeping next to her most of all. Burying his nose in her hair. Spooning heated flesh against heated flesh. The slow pulse of breath and heart a soothing lullaby that had given him the most restful nights of sleep he'd known and allowed him to forget— if only for a bit—his failures.

When had the shift happened?

Dead leaves swished against the tin roof in mocking whispers.

With a decisive roll toward the wall, he turned his back on Nora.

Stay focused.

The voice of his take-no-bull RI from Ranger School came back to him. *What's really important here? Set your expectations.*

Find Tommy. Find the boy. Get back alive.

He couldn't afford to feel sorry for Nora. He couldn't afford to feel anything at all.

Chapter Six

Getting out of a warm sleeping bag and into the darkness before dawn was like jumping naked into an icy lake. When they'd hiked as kids, Sabriel had preferred to linger until sunlight warmed the air before venturing out, while Tommy had been the early riser, popping up to catch the first crack of light breaking over the mountains.

Sabriel whipped off the sleeping bag and forced himself into the shack's cold air. Finding Tommy would mean backtracking toward Camden, and for that, they had to be ready to meld into the landscape.

Foliage was just past peak and the yellows of the oaks and the reds of maples had dulled to russet and brown. The throngs of leaf peepers had thinned, but the cars of those who'd miscalculated their reservations would still choke I-93, the Kancamagus Highway and various secondary highways that ringed the White Mountain National Forest and the surrounding state parks. With the sun looking as if it would make an appearance today, Sunday drivers and hikers would come out in droves.

Sabriel poked into Anna's cedar-lined chest. He brought out a knit cap to cover Nora's hair and fingered the soft wool. The contents of this chest were all he had left of Anna. Her ashes had gone to her beloved sea. And brought another blast of revenge from the Colonel. No Camden—disowned or not—had been buried outside the family plot in over a hundred years.

Heart heavy, Sabriel redistributed the contents of his pack so that Nora could carry a light load with Anna's pack. Then he went out to the shed and dusted off the old Ford truck Tommy kept tuned and tanked for old-time's sake. He found the key under a rock just inside the entrance and drove the truck out to the shack, then stowed the Jeep, with its recognizable back-end damage, in the shed.

He boiled water for oatmeal, then knelt beside Nora and hesitated, loathe to wake her up. She'd tossed and turned most of the night, begging, imploring, appealing for something he couldn't quite make out—most likely her son. He'd wanted to wrap her in his arms to calm her distress, but knew it would take more than that to soothe her. Just before dawn, she'd finally stumbled into a peaceful corner of her mind and slept deeply, allowing him to catch an hour of needed rest.

For a moment, he just watched her, unable to pull his gaze from her face. A crease of worry pleated her forehead in sleep. Long lashes twitched against the fatigue-bruised skin under her eyes. Her lips moved in silent prayer, and he caught himself wanting to kiss them still.

Yeah, like that'd be a brilliant move. Divorced or not, she was still Tommy's girl—and a Camden. Operating low on sleep was obviously screwing with his mind. Which didn't bode well for the upcoming trek.

Control. Discipline. Focus. Grandpa Yamawashi and Will Daigle had patiently instilled the concepts. The Army and Ranger School had reinforced them. The Colonel and his influence had tested them to their limits.

And Nora, with her sweet almond scent, soft skin and big, brown eyes, was demolishing the careful training without even trying. Not her fault he hadn't invited a woman into his bed for far longer than was healthy.

How could he be attracted to her? A Camden? A woman who'd lead him inevitably to another showdown with the Colonel?

Your timing sucks, man.

Annoyed with himself, he reached down to her shoulder and gently shook her. "Time to get up."

She jacked upright as if he'd used a cattle prod on her, the daze of confusion clouding her eyes. "Scotty?"

"That's the plan." He pulled away before he did something stupid like hug her and tell her everything was going to be okay. "Breakfast is ready. I want to get going as soon as possible."

Questions stirred through the deep brown of her eyes, reeling him in like a hapless fish. Good thing she kept them at bay until he steered Will's truck onto a dirt track that led away from the entrance gate or he might have snapped at her just because he was mad at himself.

"Where are we going now?" Nora asked, worry underlying the careful nonchalance of her voice.

"Neighbor's drive. It'll pop us out of the backside of the lake."

"There's a lake?"

He chuckled. "Not much of a lake, I'll admit. But there is one. We'll take the back way to White Mountain Road."

And if the Colonel's goons came poking around, Will's visitor deterrent would greet them. Finding four new tires in the middle of nowhere should keep them busy for a bit. And, with any luck, he and Nora would have disappeared into the mountains, their tracks lost among the thousands of previous boot prints that had worn the Fever Trail.

"White Mountain Road?" Nora's eyes widened to full moons. "But we can't go back that way. The Colonel—"

"It's where Tommy's trail starts. Six point six miles from the Smiling Moose Café."

She sucked in a breath and murmured, "Route 66."

He nodded.

"The rest? What did it mean?"

She watched him as if he were an oracle, her breath hanging on his ability to divine, and he couldn't help the tiny surge of pleasure that he could offer her some answers. "'Band on the Run' means he's running with Scotty—which you already figured out. The trailhead spears three trails. 'Deep Water' is the trail that follows the Flint River. And 'Graceland' is the White Mountain National Forest."

She gazed longingly at the mountains. A measure of

awe and fear gave her voice a breathy quality that sang into his bones. "Somewhere in there. That's where we'll find them."

"We will find them," he said and surprised himself with the sureness of his proclamation.

Once they hit the highway, she gripped the seat as if she expected him to push a button and eject her at any second. Her gaze darted back and ahead, no doubt searching for a black Hummer—or two, or three.

"The Colonel will be watching for us," she said, blushing when he caught her vigilance.

"For the Jeep. We'll just be two hikers."

"Right." But her fingers, knitting themselves into a snarl, betrayed her doubt.

As they neared the trailhead, Sabriel widened the perimeter of his vision, conscious of every sound and scent and sight. He took in the almost full parking lot; the groups of twos and fours, chatting, gathering up gear and checking the map on the board near the fork that speared in three directions; the goons stationed at both ends of the lot, disguised as hikers. His heightened senses also burned with awareness of Nora beside him—her fears, hopes and worries writhing out from her in heated snakes.

Hang in there, girl. All you have to do is follow my lead. He resisted the temptation to reach for her hand and stroke it.

As he turned into the parking lot, she gasped and shrank down in her seat, vibrating with tension that threatened to crack her. "That's Boggs!"

"You've got to relax, Nora." Sabriel nosed into one of the two remaining spaces and killed the engine. "We're just two hikers out for a day trip. Smile. You're supposed to be having fun."

The wobbly number she pulled out wasn't going to do the job.

"Come on," he urged. "You can do better than that. For Scotty."

She blew out a breath and nodded. "I can do this. I can pretend I'm a seasoned hiker."

"I wouldn't go that far," he teased.

She exploded in shaky laughter. "Didn't you know? Being a nervous wreck is my natural state."

"Then we'll make full use of your abilities." He smiled and she smiled back—a real smile that buzzed unexpected warmth into his solar plexus. "Come on. Let's get this show on the road."

She turned and reached for the door handle, but he held her back and shoved a stray strand of her rich brown hair back into the navy cap, searching for words of reassurance. Ah, hell. Not a good sign. She wasn't his friend. He needed to keep his distance or he'd never make it back in one piece.

"Put on your shades," he said, leaning away from the lure of her scent. "There are three of the Colonel's men hanging around. Boggs to our right on the other side of the trailhead." The other two he recognized from the pictures in the personnel file Kingsley had forwarded to his PDA. "Hutt is to our left, five cars down." Like a vulture, Hutt circled closer for a better look. "And

Costlow is pretending to be reading the map at the trail-head. When we go by him, I'm going to say something in French. When I stop talking, giggle, okay?"

"You know French?"

At least she wasn't questioning the plan. "One of my grandfathers is French Canadian. The group of four that was parked next to us was speaking French. We'll pretend we're with their party. Ready?"

She gulped and nodded. He kept his body between her and Boggs's view as he adjusted the pack on her back.

Hutt pulled up close and drew a cigarette from a pack in his breast pocket. "Got a light?"

"Ah, non," Sabriel said with a heavy French accent. *"No smoke."*

Hutt stared, no doubt hoping to intimidate. *Stare all you want, buddy. All you're gonna see in my mirrored shades is your own reflection.*

Nora started to fidget, then tugged on his sleeve and said, *"Eh, on y va?"*

Well, well, Nora had a few surprises of her own.

Hutt's gaze flicked between them before he stepped back to his post.

As Sabriel and Nora strolled onto the trail, Costlow looked up from his map and nodded a greeting.

"Salut." Sabriel waved at him and wrapped one hand around Nora's. Her fingers shook against his and he gave them a little squeeze.

He pulled her intimately close, and bent down to tell her one of his grandfather's bad jokes in French as if he were showering her with sweet nothings. Right on cue, she giggled. A little forced, but good enough to have Costlow dismiss them and scan over their shoulders into the parking lot.

A spurt of triumph raced through his blood. She'd done it. She'd kept her cool and fooled the Colonel's men, who saw her every day.

The trail wound and turned, climbing northeast and skirting the rushing Flint River for the first mile through beeches, maples and hemlocks, then broke away to cut more steeply through rocky terrain. Wind gusted in small puffs, streaming through the russets, reds and browns of the woods. A hawk slid through the air above almost flush with the mountain's side, then it dove out of sight.

Costlow followed at a distance, but Sabriel didn't alter his leisurely pace. As the forest's Web site had predicted, the ground was saturated with water and held on to their tracks. That was going to be a problem once they left the trail.

"How did they know where to look?" Nora asked, puffing out the question as if it had been jumping around in her mouth for the last mile.

"Maybe they spotted the vehicle Tommy used to get there."

"I didn't see his Jeep."

"He could've borrowed or rented something else." Sabriel slanted her a curious glance. "You know French?"

She shrugged. "Couldn't do math worth a darn in school, but I picked up languages fast. French, German, Spanish. I've always wanted to travel."

Not this way, he'd bet. For someone with wanderlust,

the Colonel's mansion must have felt doubly like a prison. Why had she stayed there so long? *None of your business, buster.*

He could see her in the vineyards of France, the coast of Spain, the Black Forest of Germany, soaking in all the local flavors like a sea sponge. She looked like the type who wouldn't stick to the tourist routes, but explore side roads, making the trip exciting for anyone who'd lucked into tagging along.

He shook his head and readjusted his pack. *Yeah, right, and you know that how?*

They trekked along a section of deadwood, probably blown down by a storm, bare trunks lying across each other like a giant game of pick-up sticks. A little farther up dead snags, still standing, mixed with new trees—the forest regenerating itself. Heading into the mountains usually felt that way, like a regeneration, a filling of spirit.

Not today. Not with Nora a target. A liability. His responsibility. A shiver ran through him as if a bank of clouds had blown across the sun.

Forty feet farther up the trail, Sabriel spotted Tommy's first sign, pointing them into the woods. A big toe-shaped rock stuck on a tulip-shaped leaf. "Tiptoe Through the Tulips." A smile wobbled on his lips. Tommy's bizarre sense of humor in action. He wanted them to track through the deadwood. The blister on the leaf indicated the direction and position of the next sign.

With Nora's inexperience outdoors, ditching their tail wasn't going to be a breeze. This chase, this action, this *hunt* was what the Colonel had trained his goons for.

Costlow wouldn't fool or give up easily. Not with the scent of possible blood in the air.

Sporting a lover's smile, which came much too effortlessly when he looked into her eyes, Sabriel turned to Nora. He bent down toward her as if to kiss her, felt the twitch of desire ripple through his gut, and whispered, "This is where we leave the trail. We just have to take care of our escort first."

NORA'S HEART kicked into high gear. After they'd gone by the last of the Colonel's men at the trailhead, she'd thought their ruse had worked and they'd left all three thugs behind. She jerked her head toward the trail behind them, but Sabriel held her face in place with the tips of his fingers, rough on the sensitive skin of her jaw.

"Don't look." The tranquil green of his eyes held her in thrall like a hypnotist's pendulum. His gentle smile and the calm tone of his voice quieted the flutters in her stomach.

"Someone's following us?" To her horror, her voice squeaked. "But how? We fooled them."

"Just Costlow. He was probably told to track any man-woman team for a short distance."

"Is he going to be a problem?"

His smile widened. "Not when I'm done with him."

Dragging in a breath, she nodded. Playing along with his lover's ploy, she looped her arms around his neck, fighting her need to plaster herself against him and drink in his confidence. "He has a gun."

"He's not going to want to attract attention while

other hikers are around. There's still cell reception here. He can't afford to have the authorities mixed up in this." Sabriel brushed his lips against hers to give the illusion of a kiss and her mouth fell open, craving a taste. "He's still checking things out. He needs privacy."

Not as reassuring as she would have liked. Finding her balance, she let her hands slip from his neck, missing his solid warmth. "Once he figures it out, he'll have a starting point. He'll call the others. They could get to Scotty first."

"We don't have to hand him a map." Sabriel set off, holding her hand firmly in his. "Pretend you're fascinated by the scenery." He grinned crookedly. "Or me."

Her head roared with a rush of blood. Under different circumstances, he would fascinate her. The dark, exotic looks. The wild green of his eyes. The contrast of savage vitality and wry humor. Her pulse sobered. All she could think of now was Scotty. Finding him and keeping him from the Colonel.

And since Sabriel had pointed out the thug's presence, his preylike energy hooked the back of her neck like leeches. The trail up ahead curved into a bend, and she couldn't wait to break the sticky hold.

Sabriel caught her elbow, his fingers transmitting both reassurance and urgency. "Stay an arm's length behind me and follow my every footstep."

Just before the bend, Sabriel left the trail as if he planned on cutting the corner. "This way."

Nora plunged into the thick undergrowth right behind him. This did not seem like a good plan. They were going even slower now, giving Costlow a chance to catch up.

Around a maple thicker than her arm span, Sabriel did some sort of fancy footwork that made the seconds tick by with molasses slowness. Costlow's black fleece bobbed through the woods, and Nora turtled into her jacket, seeking to make the smallest possible target.

She drew her lips in, biting down on them to keep her questions trapped so her voice wouldn't beam their position like a clarion. Ha! As if her voice would matter with her footsteps stirring dead leaves into a mad frenzy.

Sabriel zigzagged, twisted and veered, and she struggled to keep up. You'd think she weighed a thousand pounds with the racket she was making. What was he thinking?

Away from the trail—she sucked at distances—he shifted direction again, forty-five degrees to the right. Then started walking in a way that would double them back on their own trail.

Hurried footsteps and frustrated curses echoed somewhere behind them. "I need backup."

Oh, great, Sabriel's maneuvers had given them away. For all she knew, Costlow had still thought they were French before Sabriel acted oddly enough to attract attention.

At the edge of the trail, using a fat oak for camouflage, Sabriel paused and scanned the area, then burst onto the trail and into the blinding sunlight, making her blink. He was heading in the direction they'd just evaded. This was crazy. He was trying to get them caught.

She jabbed him with her elbow, frowning fiercely, and silently asked him what was going on.

He shook his head, but didn't elaborate. He looked up and down at their tracks, then slowed and walked backward, signaling her to do the same.

Where granite poked through the thin skin of earth, Sabriel dodged left, on the opposite side of the trail, taking them into the tangle of dead trees that looked ready to break ankles.

Moving as silently and as smoothly as a fox, setting a fast pace, but adjusting for her slower gait, he slid between impossible gaps, squeezed past trunks, snaked around boulders, crawled under branches. While she crashed behind him like a drunken squirrel, chugging breaths as loudly as a steam locomotive. How was that going to fool Costlow?

The dead strangle of downed trees gave way to forest and the trees choked around them as if they would never let them go. A maze with no exit.

Sweat poured down her torso, chafing her skin under the pack's strap with every step. She whipped a frantic glance toward the marked trail they'd left only minutes ago. Damp leaves glittered like pennies in the sun, shimmering the tree trunks around her in a mirage that transformed the landscape into something as alien as Saturn.

One truth mushroomed with each of her labored breaths. She could not crack this wilderness code alone. If anything happened to Sabriel, she would be profoundly lost.

She didn't like being so dependent on him. On anyone. In this thick vastness of the outdoors, she realized just how bleak a prison she'd made for herself and for Scotty at the mansion. Rather than prepare herself for independence after the divorce, she'd hung on like some sort of remora on a shark. She'd done so with good intentions, for Scotty's sake, but everybody knew what road good intentions paved.

At least the trail behind them was deserted. Had they lost Costlow?

"Looking back like that—" Sabriel signaled toward the tube attached to the water bladder in her pack and took a sip from his own. "That's good. People get lost because they don't look back to see how things would look on the way home."

She was in the belly of a magnificent, dangerous and unpredictable beast. It could swallow her up without a burp. *Please, Tommy, keep Scotty safe.*

"Being scared isn't a weakness," Sabriel said, striding forward again, climbing around a tumble of boulders. "It's facing reality. You're out of your element here. It should scare the crap out of you."

"You must have failed Comfort 101."

He laughed and the sound was so unexpected and rich that it tripped an echoing rattle in her gut that had nothing to do with the rough terrain. "Yeah, but I aced survival school."

Knowing that was true helped calm her. "How do you know where to go?"

"I can read the signs Tommy and Scotty left behind."

"I don't see anything."

"Wherever you go, you leave a trace." He stopped and, using his finger as a pointer, he drew a snaking line in the air to the rising terrain ahead. "Tommy's path is steady. There, Scotty skips ahead. He stops there, probably to check out a bug on the rock. He sat there on that jut. Tommy sat next to him on the fallen log. Looks like they had some trail mix. There's a half a peanut and a raisin on the ground."

"You can see all that?" And she saw nothing. Was he making this up to make her feel better? She knuckled the bony joint between her breasts. It didn't matter. She'd take his tale—lie or truth. Scotty was alive. He was healthy. He was happy. And Tommy was taking good care of him.

Sabriel turned her around, the hard length of his body a comforting brace behind her. "Look where you've been. Can you see the crushed vegetation? The imprint of your boot in the moss? The scratch of your pack on that birch?"

She frowned. The tiny fresh scar on the white flesh, maybe. But the others?

"It took me a lot of dirt time to learn," he said. "All it takes is practice."

Sure. Easy for him to say. But she didn't have time to practice.

She nevertheless hung on to the image of Scotty skipping, safe in Tommy's care, and pushed on, concentrating on putting one foot in front of the other on the moist leaf litter that sucked at her boots.

The silence between her and Sabriel grew as she focused on following his footsteps in the ever changing, yet indistinguishable, landscape.

The smell of evergreen and moss and a biting kind of spiciness that was unique to wilderness scented the air. Giant boulders, strewn cascades of rocks and trip wires of roots bulging out of the sparse ground all conspired to make her stumble on a regular basis.

They came to a slope that seemed to have carved high steps out of the granite. The rock was slick with a trickle of water and her boots scuffed along the slippery surface. She fell down hard on one knee, letting out an *oomph* of breath.

Sabriel reached for her hand, helping her up the odd staircase. A man's hand, strong and rough. As soon as she was over the obstacle, he dropped his hand, but its warmth lingered against her palm.

What was wrong with her? How could she think of Sabriel as a man when her son was in danger?

Survival, she thought. Her life and her son's depended on this man. Forming a bond of trust was normal, necessary even. Hadn't she done the same to survive the streets of Boston after her mother had dumped her?

On the rising ground, her ankles rolled through every possible contortion of their joint. Her feet were so hot they felt on fire. So were her lungs. The pack's straps cut into her shoulders, numbing them.

Still, she soldiered on. She wasn't going to complain. She wasn't going to make Sabriel regret he took her along. They would find Scotty. Soon. Safe. And somehow she would find a way to save him from the Colonel.

The trees thinned and they came to a flat expanse of

bare rock that provided the first view of their upcoming journey. The vast breadth of boundless sky stole her breath away and stamped her mind with the impossibility of the task ahead of them.

All those trees. All those cliffs. All those mountains. Ridge after ridge of them. Even living in their shadows for eleven years had not prepared her for how far the White Mountains stretched out. Her heart kicked. Scotty might as well be a needle in the haystack of these endless woods.

"We'll find them," Sabriel said as if he could read her mind.

"It's so…big."

"Tommy's leaving us the map."

Nodding, she willed her mind to slow and not jump straight to the worst-case scenario. Sabriel could read the map. He would find them. She had to trust.

Sabriel slipped off his pack and dug out his small stove and a couple of packets of dried soup.

She hated to stop and give the thug a chance to catch up to them. But her energy was flagging and she understood that rest and food would allow her to trek on longer.

She shed her pack and let it drop on the slant of rock. Pinched nerves rebounded, tingling life back into her shoulders. Fatigue settled into her limbs like an anchor. "Can I help?"

"I've got it under control."

"Back there?" she asked, closing her eyes against the too-broad view that heightened her sense of helplessness. "On the trail where we lost the Colonel's man? What did you do?"

He stirred hot water into the soup mix in cups and handed her one. The scent of chicken broth wafted to her nose and set her stomach grumbling. "Moving across an area without leaving signs is almost impossible. Especially if the tracker following us has any skill."

"But I thought you and Tommy were good at disappearing." She stirred the noodles into an eddy.

He handed her a pack of cheese-and-peanut-butter crackers. "Hiding our trail would take too much time. Especially with our packs. We couldn't outrun Costlow, traveling light like he was. That left deception techniques."

"So we're safe now?" Costlow's sticky vibe hadn't grabbed for her neck in a while.

"At best all we managed to do was confuse him."

Though she shivered at the thought of the thug still on their trail, she was glad Sabriel wasn't whitewashing the gravity of their situation to spare her feelings.

He took her empty cup and handed her a Jonagold apple.

She hadn't realized how hungry she was and an apple had never tasted so good—crisp like the sunny autumn day, tart like the breeze; the sweetest thing she'd ever eaten.

Then the image of Scotty on their outing to an orchard—was it only a month ago?—flashed into her memory. How he'd had such a good time filling their bag with Macintosh, Macoun and Cortland apples. How his tongue had poked out the side of his mouth as he'd concentrated on the heavy picker to reach the biggest, highest apple on a Macintosh tree. How he'd devoured his treasure on the spot, his chin dripping with juice.

Was Scotty getting enough to eat? The tender flesh of the Jonagold stuck in her throat.

"By now the other goons will have run the truck's plates and figured out we're who they're looking for," Sabriel said, gaze on the woods from where they'd come. "We can expect more company."

"Can't your Seekers friend help you? Can't they stop them?"

"We need them back there, gathering intelligence and evidence. Seekers, Inc. is a private organization. We don't have arrest authority. We have to work through other law enforcement agencies."

Sabriel stood abruptly, alert as a deer scenting a coyote. A faraway noise, like the bugle of a ghoul, rose above the treetops and shot an electric eel of alarm up her spine.

"What's that?" she asked, every instinct shouting at her to flee.

"A tracking dog."

Chapter Seven

Nora sprang up from the rock where she'd been sitting and swept up her backpack. Her breathing exploded into a ragged whisper. "Dogs? As in a bloodhound that can track our scent?"

"Sounds more like a German shepherd," Sabriel said, voice as steady as the rock on which they stood. He scoured the landscape below them. "Probably an air-scent dog."

Nora swung to face him, a brick of panic weighing her chest. "What does that mean?"

"For us? Not much. Either way the dog'll latch on to our scent."

That did not sound good. "How much time to we have?"

"They're about half a mile back." Sabriel frowned. He sank down on the rock as if they had all the time in the world and asked for her pack.

"Shouldn't we get moving? Fast?"

"I want to pool our scent." He wrenched the pack from her tight grip and proceeded to empty it.

He knew what he was doing. She shouldn't question him, but… "Are you crazy?"

"It'll make the dog pay attention to this spot."

Her voice climbed through the tight rope of her throat. "Isn't the idea to make sure that it doesn't?"

"I'm going to confuse him."

"How?"

"Olfactory overload."

Sabriel ignored Anna's belongings, but zeroed in on the purse Nora had insisted on bringing, rifling through its contents with meticulous care. "What are you looking for?"

"They found us way too fast."

"You're thinking the Colonel put a tracking device on me?"

Sabriel didn't answer, but took apart her cell phone, her keychain and the lining of her purse.

She wrung her empty hands. "Then why didn't his men get us last night?"

"I don't know."

And the admission cost him. "They were at the trail-head this morning. How did they know to start there? The Colonel didn't see the note."

"The Colonel isn't stupid. He's figured—just like you did—that Tommy went to the mountains. But even the Colonel doesn't have unlimited resources. He didn't know which trail Tommy took. He had to wait for us to show him."

Standing like this, Nora feared she would fall to pieces, the sounds of dog and men—at least two distinct voices—bounced against trees and granite, reverberating like thunder, getting closer, rattling at her already clanging nerves. She'd led them here, to Tommy, to Scotty. If the goons got to Scotty before she could, it would be her fault. How long would it take the tracker and his dog to catch up? To latch on to Scotty's scent?

Her son's smile rose up in her mind and her vision went hot and blurry. Was Tommy lucid enough to fight for Scotty, to protect him against the danger gaining on them?

She couldn't let the Colonel's men stop her. She would not fall prey to a convenient accident. She had to remain Scotty's champion. "Hurry. *Please*. We can't stay here."

"Hey." Sabriel stood and tapped the side of his hand gently against her chin. "It's going to be okay."

More than anything, she wanted to believe in the confidence reflected in his green eyes, in him. "We should go. Now. Before they find us."

He opened his palm, revealing two black dots the size of a sharpened pencil lead.

"What are those?"

"Microdots." Sabriel unknotted the black bandanna at his throat and carefully wrapped the microdots. "They're being tested by the Army as a way to locate soldiers downed in battle. The Colonel could have gotten his hands on some through his lab's R & D department."

"Wouldn't something that small be useless out here? We're so far from everything." How long had they been planted in her things? How long had the Colonel been keeping track of her every intimate movement? The thought made the hair on the back of her neck ripple with a chill. Fears weren't paranoia if they proved true.

"On a battlefield, the range has to be far and broad. Reed, the guy who was getting married when you called, almost lost Abbie, the girl he married, because her stalker was using microdots to track her. And they were running all over New England."

Sabriel crooked a finger in a come-closer gesture. "I'm not getting fresh, but I need to see if there are any more of these on you."

She plucked at the polypropylene base layer. "Everything I'm wearing belongs to Anna."

An almost imperceptible flash of pain flinched through his eyes, then steadied as if bringing up his dead wife's name shouldn't be allowed to hurt. *You loved her,* she wanted to say. *It should hurt.* He studied her with X-ray-visionlike intensity, making her wish for a lead shield. "There's your bra."

Heat fired up her neck. "Wouldn't he have to replace the dots every time I washed it?"

His index finger pressed against the lump between her breasts—the oval locket Tommy had given her at Scotty's birth—and made her aware of the pulse pumping through her heart. The locket held a picture of Scotty as a newborn and another of her son she changed every year.

"May I?"

The touch of his fingers on her nape, as he worked at unclasping the chain, jolted through her faster than the strong coffee the Colonel favored, wreaking havoc on her senses. She squirmed at the unanticipated rush of pleasure arrowing straight to her stomach. How could his nearness punch her with such lust when Scotty was missing and a tracking dog was minutes away from ripping them to pieces? She reached up to push the torture of his hands away from her neck. "I can do it."

"I've got it."

The chain parted. Their gazes met and the air between them spiked with something she didn't want to acknowledge. He quickly broke the spell, taking a step back, and cracked open the locket in the cushion of his palm.

Behind her son's baby picture, Sabriel harvested a third dot.

She snapped a nervous laugh, trying to stay as calm as he was, trying to make sense of the madness festering in every facet of her life. "How low can the man go?"

"He's not used to losing, and you refuse to fall completely under his control." Sabriel handed her the locket, then crouched next to his pack, removed the food from the bear bag until he'd lined up a handful of small fast-food restaurant pepper packages. He ripped them open and dumped the contents on the clump of moss where they'd sat.

"What are you doing?" Nora worked at fastening the locket around her neck. Her shaking fingers couldn't connect the clasp to the ring, and she finally gave up, shoving the gold oval and chain into the pocket of her pants.

"One whiff of the pepper and the dog won't be able to smell for hours. That should be long enough for us to gain some ground." Sabriel stuffed the empty wrappers into his pack, then stowed her belongings back into her pack and hiked it onto her shoulders. He handed her a clove of garlic. "Suck on this."

"Why?"

"It'll help mask your scent." He pointed back into the woods, up where the mountain crested. "I want you to head that way. It's downwind and will minimize point smells."

"You're not coming with me?" Nora's hands gripped the straps of her pack into tight fists, paralyzed.

Ignoring her question, his finger moved to an oak near the top of the rise. "See that tree with the bump that looks like a seal's head?"

Gulping, she nodded.

"When you get there, look to the right for a deer run and keep following it up for a quarter mile, then down until you reach the stream."

Her heart stormed. Her blood thundered. "Alone?"

"I'm going to give them something to look for." He held up the bandanna.

"But—"

"You'll be okay. I'll catch up with you."

I can't. I can't. I can't. "I'll get lost."

"I'll find you."

"I—"

He cocked his head. Voice commands of handler to dog strafed the air like buckshot. "Hear that? That's the Colonel's men. They'll be there in less than five minutes." He shrugged. "Your choice."

She opened her mouth, but no sound came out.

"Go on. *Move.*" Sabriel's predatory gaze, hawk-sharp and eagle-bold, made her shiver. This was not a man to mess with. She almost felt sorry for the Colonel's men.

Leaving his pack behind near the pepper-baited spot, Sabriel steered toward their pursuers. The crash of men through the woods drew closer and closer, jagging her pulse in a demented reel.

Come on, Nora. Move. Sabriel's doing his part. Time to do yours.

Screwing up her courage, she popped the clove of garlic into her mouth and sprinted uphill toward the seal-head tree, willing her feet to go faster, praying for Sabriel's safety, keeping Scotty—her goal—in her mind's eye.

A root buried in the litter caught her foot, and she plowed facedown into dry leaves. Searching for her vanished breath, she scrambled to her feet. A quick glance behind showed her flashes of movement. Thug or beast? Sabriel? She couldn't tell.

Move, Nora, move.

Thigh muscles trembling, she took off again. Breathing hard, she reached the tree with the seal-shaped lump. She rested a hand against the deformity and caught her breath. Shifting her gaze to the right, she searched for the deer path, saw nothing but leaf litter and a tight net of tree trunks.

Tears rose up, clogged her throat. *Useless. You're nothing but useless. You can't protect your only child. You can't find a damned deer path to save his life.*

If she lost Scotty, nothing would matter. She couldn't give up.

Frantic, she scoured the woods, getting down on hands and knees, furrowing through the leaf decay like a dervish. The dog's howls reached near orgasmic rapture and wrapped around in surround sound hyper-reality. Where was Sabriel?

In her frenzy, her wrist caved into a dip in the ground, unbalancing her. She brushed aside some leaves and found an old track—two half moons kissing to form a heart. Even she'd seen deer tracks in the snow behind the estate.

A thrill rushed through her. *I found it!*

She corralled her joyful shout with her hand and stepped onto the track. Keeping her gaze fixed on the dips in the leaves marking the trail, she followed one indentation to the next, up and up and up until the trail took a sharp downward shift and the gurgle of a stream filtered above the shouts and barks of men and dogs.

Keep going, Nora. You can do this.

As she tired, her shirt snagged on branches and her boots gouged the leaf litter, turning the dried leaves over to display their damp undercover.

Might as well paint an arrow, she thought with a sneer.

Distance, that's all that mattered. *Get away from the dogs. Get to the stream.* Sabriel would know what to do next.

Just as her pulse finally evened, the report of a gun echoed in the woods, surrounding her with a deafening boom. Her feet froze. Shaking, she whirled around to face the direction of the shot.

Sabriel?

Her breath chugged. Her heart rattled against her ribs. Was he hurt? Should she go back? If she did, she'd land right into the hands of the Colonel's men and Scotty would become the Colonel's captive.

But what if Sabriel needed help? He'd gone out of his way to help her. She couldn't just leave him there to die.

He knows the woods. He knows how to survive.

But even he couldn't outrun a bullet.

A strangled sound escaped her. She spun around, searching through the blur of trees for an answer. *Please, someone, help me!*

The choked plea turned into caustic laughter. *Who is there to help you, Nora? You're in the middle of a forest. You're on your own. You're going to have to help yourself if you want to save Scotty.*

She'd keep going, make it to the rendezvous point, then she'd decide what to do next.

Move, Nora, move.

Sabriel, please, please be okay.

Her heavy legs balked at first, then obeyed her command. The terrain shifted, plunging her down a steep incline studded with knobby knuckles of rocks. She slipped on a slick of wet granite, landed on her butt and slid down the ravine. She threw her arms out like ballasts, praying she didn't tumble and break something. Somehow she managed to push herself up to her feet and scrambled down the rest of the way to the stream.

This deep under the thick canopy of trees, the slant of the sun's rays had weakened, leaving long shadows that shifted and stalked. Breath churning in her lungs, she took stock of her surroundings. The stream ran only two feet wide and no more than a foot deep. The small clearing left her exposed, an open target.

What was she supposed to do now? She rolled the clove of garlic in her mouth. What if something had happened to Sabriel? How was she supposed to help him if she didn't know where he was? How was she supposed to find Scotty in this no-man's-land?

Even though her body steamed like hot coffee, the rising cold breeze dried her sweat and gooseflesh beetled her skin. She put on the fleece jacket Sabriel had stuffed in her pack and zipped it up all the way to her chin.

Where are you, Sabriel?

The longer she waited, the more her mind infected her with doubt, raising red flags of fear that flapped with dread. What if the thugs had killed Sabriel? What if the dog hadn't fallen for the pepper trap? How long did she have before they found Scotty?

If you keep this up, you're going to drive yourself crazy.

She couldn't let the Colonel's men trap her like some sort of scared rabbit. Hide. She had to hide. A denned rabbit survived. And as long as she was alive, she could plan, she could look, she could have a chance to find her son.

Huddled in a ball behind a nest of rocks, hands pressed against the roil of her stomach, she irrationally wanted her mother. Someone to hold her and tell her everything was going to be all right. Not that her mother had ever been there for her, but that didn't seem to matter in this off-balance, twilight zone world. She wanted the comfort of arms around her.

The memory of Sabriel's strong hands warmed her palm. His sure and steady gaze rippled back into her consciousness, ebbing the ferocity of her shivers.

He was alive. He was okay. He would come back and find her.

He had to. She would accept nothing else.

In the meantime, it was up to her to stay out of the path of the Colonel's men.

SABRIEL FOUND Nora by the stream, crouching behind a ring of boulders, so still and quiet, she might have been part of the scenery if it wasn't for her navy jacket and blue pack. Fear beamed from her eyes, shot like red flares. The elastic tie had fallen from her ponytail, leaving her hair in a spiked mess around her pale face.

Balled like that, she looked small and defenseless, but even trapped, her face showed the grit of determination. The porcelain skin hid steel he'd bet even she didn't know was there, and that quiet courage tugged at him.

Don't let her get to you, man. You can't afford to want someone the Colonel can use against you.

She had no idea he was only a few yards from her, hidden by the trees. No matter how he showed himself, he'd startle her.

He crashed out of the woods, at an angle so she would easily see him. At the sound of his boots on the leaves, she tightened the spring of her body, rolled on the balls of her feet, ready to bolt.

Halfway out of her crouch, she recognized him and relief swam through her wide eyes, flowed down her shoulders. "You're okay."

"Why wouldn't I be?"

Even as she rose, her breaths came in the choppy bursts of rattled nerves. She staggered a little as if she'd forgotten she wore a pack on her back. He steadied her, the small bones of her forearm fragile in his palm.

"The gunshot…I thought…" She shoved her hands into her hair and pulled at the crown of her head as if she was going to yank the brown strands out. "I thought they'd shot you. I thought you were hurt, maybe dead."

His arms hitched in rescue mode, but he stopped them before they pulled her to him to absorb the tremor of her shock into his chest. *Way to keep your distance, man. You can't save her any more than you could save Anna. Stick to the mission.* "You don't have much confidence in me."

"I do. I do." She closed her eyes, folded her arms over her chest and shook her head. The vibrations of her emotions rolled deep into his gut. "I didn't know if I should stay, if I should go."

"You did just fine." Better than he'd expected. "You found the stream. You crossed on the rocks. And you picked a good place to watch and wait."

She nodded, her voice calmer now. "I did."

She lifted those big, brown eyes up at him, and he swallowed back the sudden urge to kiss her. "Why did they shoot?"

"They killed the dog." A bloody mess he wouldn't soon wipe from his mind. Such a damned waste.

Her eyes widened and her mouth gaped open. "Why?"

"He wasn't of any more use to them." His jaw flinched. So little respect for life.

"But he was trained—"

"With his nose out of commission, he couldn't track. Taking him back would have taken too long." Another miscalculation on his part. "We need to get going."

"Because of us. They killed him because of us."

Sabriel turned away from the naked horror in her eyes and lifted the pack onto his shoulders. "It also bought us time to find Scotty."

"I didn't want anybody to get hurt."

"Then let's not waste his sacrifice," Sabriel said, and couldn't quite tamp down the cold edge of his guilt. "Let's go. Daylight's almost gone, and we have a lot of ground to cover."

SABRIEL STRODE into the woods, and Nora followed. They climbed up the ravine, using switchbacks carved by the deer to ease the strain of the rise. The trail leveled off to a ledge with overgrown views of Mt. Washington.

There he found Tommy's next sign. The crude tattoo of a mountain and valley on a leaf skewered by a stick pitchfork and held in place by an egg-shaped rock. "The Farmer in the Dell."

Sabriel grinned. He'd thought old man Wagner would have been dead by now. He'd looked a hundred years old seventeen years ago. He couldn't imagine how the farmer was still milking cows and collecting eggs.

Was he still plowing his field with the Clydesdale that had to be as ancient as he was?

Nora walked behind Sabriel in a quiet that was too introspective. Never good, he'd learned from experience. That's when the mind twisted things around, made you question yourself. They had at least three miles before they reached the Wagner farm and not much light to get there with.

Keep her moving. Keep her too busy to worry about the dead dog, what the Colonel's men were up to or the fact that he'd taken her no closer to her son than she'd been this morning. He lengthened his stride. "Pick up the pace."

She kept up like a seasoned soldier, wringing another notch of admiration out of him that he didn't want to give.

She's not your type, he reminded himself. No, these days he preferred women whose BlackBerries were jam-packed with meetings and action items and to-do lists, leaving them with little time or desire for strings, which suited him fine.

The grade of the descent through an old strand of red spruce lessened. Nora's tired feet managed the rock-strewn and rooty ground and her breath evened out.

"I'm a liability," she said.

She'd been one from the moment she'd called in Tommy's chip. But Sabriel wasn't going to tell her that. Or how much the Colonel still wanted to destroy him. He gave an absent grunt that was neither agreement nor denial and swore he could feel her body brace behind him.

"How much of a liability am I?"

He shot her a look. "You're safe with me."

Her head dropped to her chest. "I'm sorry."

"What the hell for?"

"I never thought looking for Scotty would get so…complicated."

"With the Colonel, nothing's simple." Or maybe everything was too simple. His way or the highway. And his way wasn't always what was best for the other parties involved.

Anna's face materialized in Sabriel's mind. Her blue eyes, so sad the last time he'd kissed her.

I'm sorry, she'd whispered as she'd broken the embrace. And it had whispered across his heart like ice.

The Colonel can't get to you, Anna. You're safe with me.

He should know better than to make a promise he couldn't keep.

BY THE TIME Nora and Sabriel skirted the bog and reached the edge of the meadow, daylight had faded to night, deepening the shadows of the forest into a living, breathing thing that seemed to snap at Nora's heels. The day noises of birds and breeze quieted, giving way to night's creaks and cracks that were a sharp fingernail along her spine. A three-quarter moon rose, silvering the ground to light their way, but didn't lessen the sensation of being hunted.

Every muscle in Nora's body ached. Her thighs trembled with fatigue. Her feet were so hot, she thought they might spontaneously combust. And she could no longer feel her shoulders from the weight of the pack.

Sabriel halted in the shadow of trees, spying at the

faded white farmhouse and equally faded white barn that stood in the center, surrounded by a crosshatch of faded wood fences. "We're going to spend the night in that barn. But we have to wait until the farmer's asleep."

"Is it safe?"

"It's shelter."

Squatting wasn't new territory—just one she'd never thought she'd revisit. He was right. She wasn't in a position to complain. A barn wasn't a hotel or even a B&B, but it was better than the wide outdoors, with its wild, hungry beasts.

She batted away the unwanted image of Scotty trapped in a bobcat's fangs and slid her pack gingerly from her shoulders, wincing when the edge of the strap dug into a raw patch of skin.

"What's wrong?" Sabriel eased the pack the rest of the way down her arms.

"Nothing."

He edged aside the fleece jacket, prodded the tender skin through her shirt and swore. "You're bleeding. Why didn't you say anything?"

"I didn't want to slow us down."

He nudged her down on a rock, yanked one of her boots and socks off, and examined her foot by flashlight. "Hell, Nora, how can you even walk? If you speak up, we can readjust things before you start hurting. Once you're hurting, you slow us down."

She curled her naked foot away from his burning touch. "I didn't want to complain."

His eyes fired with jags of lightning in the moon's

light. "There's a difference between whining and taking care of yourself. There's no clinic or doctor out here. If you get hurt, we'll have to stop."

"No! We can't. Not until we find Scotty."

"Then you'll have to speak up for yourself. Your shoulders are bloody from your pinching pack. That's an invitation for an infection. Your feet are on the edge of blistering, and with blistered feet, you can't walk."

"Okay, okay. I get it." Had her stubborn determination to say nothing put finding Scotty in jeopardy?

"Anywhere else that hurts?" Sabriel asked.

She swallowed hard, loathe to add more of her burden to his overloaded shoulders. Her hands cupped her throbbing kneecaps. "Knees. Going down was a lot rougher on them than going up."

He jerked off his pack, searched its contents and brought out a first aid kit. He handed her four small white tablets. "Dissolve those under your tongue. It'll help with the sore muscles and bruising."

She popped them under her tongue, and he moved to her feet, slathering them with a gel that cooled and soothed. She nearly moaned from the sweet release of blistering pain. "That feels good."

"Put some on your knees." He tossed her the tube.

She rubbed gel around her aching knees. "What is it?"

"A homeopathic medicine."

"Where did you learn about this stuff?"

"My grandparents run an alternative health clinic." The corners of his mouth turned up, softening the angles of his face and lighting his eyes with a purity of emotions she couldn't remember ever seeing, except maybe in Scotty's eyes. "They're both flirting with eighty and still run around like teenagers. They'll both outlive me at the rate they're going."

"They sound like great people." Which triggered a slight case of envy. All she'd ever wanted was a family, a real family, with people who cared about each other, not destroyed each other.

"They're the best." He handed her a pair of fresh socks. "When your feet get hot tomorrow, say something and change to dry socks."

She nodded. "Okay."

After she'd put on the socks, he knelt at her side and gently pushed aside the shoulder of her shirt. He dabbed a medicated wipe on the skin the pack had rubbed raw. She sucked in a breath at the sting and tried really hard to focus on her knees, her feet, anything but the maddening rush of confusion his touch triggered. Her breath and her brain couldn't synchronize. Her nerves bumped along the rough ride of her pulse.

This was crazy. She was crazy. Her son was missing, in danger, and yet she wanted, needed the feel of Sabriel's hands on her skin. Those hands, rugged and male, as solid as the mountains all around them.

Simple survival, she chided herself. *It doesn't make you weak or needy.* But she couldn't quite shove aside the feeling that she was growing too dependent on him, on his skills, on his strength.

He was too rough, too hard to love a woman the way she ought to be cherished. The Colonel and Anna's death had done that to him, broken his soul, his heart. And yet in his hands, in the way he spoke about his grandparents, bloomed a vibrancy of life that drew her with magnetic power.

He fired up the small stove with his usual competence, prepared their evening meal with swift efficiency and handed her a pouch of chicken enchiladas. Above the smell of chili powder and cornmeal, she could make out his scent of pine and mint and the musk of hard physical work.

She shook her head, kneading her stomach with one hand against the sudden jolt of awareness. The situation was already too complicated to add sex to the mix.

"Eat. I'll be right back."

A spike of dread snaked out her arm and she grabbed on to his sleeve as he turned to leave. "What if the Colonel's men catch up?"

"I'm going to make sure they think we're somewhere else." He cupped his hands around his mouth and made a sound like a bird. "When you hear that, it'll be me, okay?"

"You need to eat, too."

Amusement—or was it annoyance?—glinted in his eyes. "I'll be right back."

Rounding over her legs for heat, she waited in the eerie dark, flinching at every rustle of leaf, at every scratch of branch, forcing herself to stay where she was and finish the enchilada mush. For Scotty, she could be brave.

To keep her growing jitters from tipping over into full-blown anxiety, she checked her purse and made sure Scotty's inhaler and Advair were still there, clutching both between her palms before returning them to the purse and the purse to the bottom of the pack where it would be safe.

Soon, baby, soon. Just hang on. Mommy's coming.

She closed off her mind to the dire possibilities her fear could conjure up of Scotty hurt, in pain, struggling for breath, and concentrated instead on listening for Sabriel's return.

But time stretched too long, chafing at her nerves. *Oh, for heaven's sake, what are you? Ten?* Irritated with herself, she fell back to an old habit she'd started when she was thirteen to cover up the sounds of her mother arguing with her latest boyfriend—making up playlists for her personal radio show.

"A Hard Day's Night," she thought with a smile. Yeah, she'd definitely start the set with that. "Pink Moon," "Purple Rain," "Paint it Black."

What seemed like an eternity later, the soft coo of Sabriel's birdcall materialized nearby. Relief melted through her bones. He was back. As quietly as a haunting spirit, he slid out of the wood, taking shape out of the shadows. His bronzed and lean-muscled forearms gleamed in the moonlight and her heart flip-flopped. Ridiculous to be so glad to see him.

"Ready?" he asked, as the last light at the house blinked out.

She nodded and followed him to the post-and-rail fence that bordered the fence, mimicking the way he moved, the way he placed his feet. Her footsteps, she noticed, weren't quite as awkward as they'd been, or as loud.

"Careful here," he whispered. "If you trip any of those electric wires riding along the fence boards, you'll not only get the shock of your life, you'll also light up the farmyard like a county fair."

With his help, she made it over the fence without blaring their presence. His hands felt sure and strong on her hips, and she thanked Tommy for sending Sabriel to her. Without him, she had no hope of finding Scotty before the Colonel.

Sabriel inched around the outside of the barn and slid the rolling door open wide enough for them to enter. Inside, the soft snorts and the munch of hay sounded so...normal, and quilted her with comfort. The body heat of cows and horses took the chill out of the air, adding another layer of coziness.

He pointed her toward a door. "There's a toilet and a sink in the utility room."

"Thanks." Running water, even cold water, seemed a true luxury after a day out in the woods. She washed up as best she could by the glow of a flashlight, stood sentinel for him while he did the same, then followed him up the creaky stairs to the loft.

He made his way to the far side of the stack of hay bales, out of sight, should anyone climb up to the loft. He loosened the contents of a bale and spread the hay near a large opening in the side of the barn roof—escape route?— then arranged their sleeping bags on top of the hay nest.

"Try to get some sleep," he said. "If we're lucky, we could catch up with Tommy by the end of the day tomorrow."

Hope sprang a fireball in her chest. "Really?"

"He's about twelve hours ahead of us."

She slithered into the sleeping bag, giddy with the promise that her son was within reach. Tomorrow she'd see Scotty again. Tomorrow she'd bring him home.

Sabriel knelt beside her head.

"What?" she asked, her mind still spinning with the thought of Scotty, finding him, holding him in her arms.

"Close your eyes and go to sleep."

Sabriel's hands hovered above her shoulders. Soon a gentle heat warmed the raw tissue and a prickling like a thousand tiny spiders reweaving the torn fabric of her abused skin. "What are you doing?"

"Reiki. Shh. Just relax."

She soon got lost in the sensation pouring out of his palms, unknotting the tight muscles all over her body until they were loose noodles, puddling deep into the sleeping bag. "I think," she said sleepily as he moved his heated hands above her knees, "I'm falling in love."

The rumble of his chuckle penetrated her gauzy consciousness. "Until you wake up, Sleeping Beauty, and realize I'm no Prince Charming."

"Hands…" Her tongue felt thick in her mouth, her brain fuzzy. "Heaven."

Just as she floated on the precipice of sleep, lights blasted on outside, shocking the barnyard with interrogation-room starkness. Gasping, she shot up. "What's going on?"

Sabriel had already moved, crouching by the loft opening, scanning the yard. "We've got company."

Chapter Eight

Not wanting to attract the farmer's attention, Sabriel clung to the shadows, mapping out escape routes should it become necessary. His perch from the loft offered him a good view of the farmhouse, but only an angled one of the section of fence where old man Wagner was heading, brandishing his shotgun, threatening to call the cops.

The Colonel's men scattered, their shadows melding back into the black void of the woods. He hoped they'd find the tracks he'd laid out for them and figure that their prey had met with the same unwelcome reception. That would afford Nora at least one good night's sleep.

The old man made the rounds, checking the perimeter of the fence around the farmyard for signs of breakage, then headed toward the barn.

"Don't move," Sabriel whispered to Nora, still sheathed in her sleeping bag. "Not a hair."

Her eyes widened in the garish light pouring through the loft opening, drawing him in dangerously. *Focus.*

The barn door rumbled. The lights along the aisle

popped on, one by one. The farmer cooed to his animals as if they were children, reassuring them that they were safe. The scuff of his boots on the concrete marked his interminable progress down the barn. A pat here. A gate opening there. The rustle of hay nets.

Then a pause where Sabriel swore he could hear the thunder of Nora's heart boom through the loft.

Shh, he mouthed. Her throat worked, but she remained as still as the hay bales surrounding her.

The rickety ladder to the loft creaked under the farmer's weight.

Sabriel melted more deeply into the shadows. A bug plopped into his hair. God, he hoped it wasn't a spider. He hated spiders. A shudder rolled through him. But he couldn't risk Nora's safety by swatting at the bug and end up with both of them looking at the wrong end of a shotgun.

The farmer leaned his weapon against a supporting beam and reached for the bale of hay in front of their hiding spot, grunting as he struggled to swing it down.

The bug crawled around Sabriel's scalp, inched along his nose, long legs popping in and out of his eyesight, revving his need to swat, spit, slap. Hell, of course it was a frigging spider.

The farmer hefted the bale, exposing the tops of their heads to the fluorescent light bleeding up from below. It stretched shadows to the ceiling—the bales, his, hers.

The spider's sticky feet ambled over Sabriel's lips. Pulse hammering madly, he screwed up his face. *Still, stay still.*

With a rasp of breath, the farmer swung the bale from the loft to the barn floor below. Dust and bits of hay flew. The bale landed with a plop. The farmer reached for the shotgun.

A muffled, thudlike *choo* came from Nora.

The farmer squinted at the shadows, shotgun swinging into position.

Sabriel shifted an arm, ready to deflect the shotgun's barrel.

The spider skittered across Sabriel's cheek. His skin prickled, quivered, itched.

The farmer leaned forward, poking the barrel of the shotgun ahead of him into the shadows.

A ginger-colored cat sprang down from the top of the pyramid of bales to the farmer's feet and rubbed against the farmer's legs with a rusty engine purr.

"You almost got yourself shot, cat," old man Wagner said, brushing an arthritic hand across the ginger fur.

The farmer took his time going down the ladder and adding hay to nets. The lights finally snapped off. The door rolled shut. Biting back a growl, Sabriel swatted at his head, desperately trying to dislodge the offensive spider.

"What's wrong?" Nora whispered, her voice tight and thready.

"Nothing," he said between clenched teeth. He could still feel the spider's legs scampering all over his hair, but couldn't see the damn thing.

"Are they gone?"

Figuring out Nora meant the Colonel's men took him a second. "They won't come back."

"Are you sure?" Her voice quavered.

"They think old man Wagner gave us the shotgun welcome, too."

"What about the farmer?"

Even with the spotlight the farmer had left burning in the yard, Sabriel couldn't find the spider's corpse. "He'll be down till dawn unless those lights pop back on."

"So we're safe?" she breathed on a long exhale.

"For now. Get some sleep."

Sabriel swatted at his shoulders. Where the hell was the spider?

"Are you okay?" she asked, curiosity now spicing her voice.

"Fine," he bit out.

He finally plucked the spider with its ugly long legs from his collar and dangled it between two fingers.

"What is it?" She rolled forward on her knees for a better look. "A spider? You're afraid of a little spider?"

He cocked an eyebrow. "It's not that little."

"Daddy longlegs are harmless."

His scowl deepened. "Better get some sleep while you can. We're leaving at dawn."

Nora fell back on her rear and laughed, a low, soft sound replete with relief. "I didn't think you were afraid of anything."

With an exaggerated shudder, he disposed the spider's carcass down the ladder. "Got bit by one of these suckers when I was a kid."

"I'm sorry," she said gently, watching him with those big, brown eyes filled with compassion as he inspected his sleeping bag for uninvited guests. "But in an odd sort of way, that spiders creep you out makes me feel better."

"Glad I could be of help." He shuffled into his sleeping bag and shut his eyes, only to have the sensation of a hundred spiders crawling all over him spring them open again.

"It takes a big man to admit his fears." She snugged deeper into her sleeping bag. "Not to let them get the better of him." A certain wistfulness laced her voice.

"Umph."

She rolled over toward him, looped one arm around his neck and pecked a kiss on his cheek. Soft, sweet and much too nice. "You're still my hero."

Now he had something else to torture his mind, and he almost wished for the phantom spider's return.

SLEEP ELUDED HIM. Sabriel spent the night in the fog of the netherworld, somewhere between dreaming and awake, where the gray shadows of his mistakes liked to parade and mock. Once Nora's breathing slowed and evened, he reached into his pack for the cedar flute he'd forgotten to take out the last time he'd hiked. In the shadow of the loft opening, watching the night stir beneath him, he fingered the flute, careful not to make a sound.

"What are you playing?" Nora asked sleepily. Still swaddled in her sleeping bag, she'd turned toward him and rested her weight on one elbow. The light of the spot outside gave her face both strength and softness and the play of contradictions stirred fascination.

He stashed the flute in his pack. "Nothing."

"It's beautiful."

"I wasn't playing."

"I heard the music of your fingering."

Sorrow blossoming into song, as Grandmother Serena would say. She'd given him his first flute for his fifth birthday—and taught him the healing comfort of music…and that of story. All it took was the smell of a campfire to bring her maple-sugar skin and smiling apple face to mind. How many nights had he spent enchanted by the music of her voice, retelling him the adventures of Gluskabe—the Abenaki trickster-hero?

"You should sleep while you can," he said.

"What about you?"

"Someone has to stand guard."

"You said we were safe." Her sleeping bag swished as she sat up. "I can take a turn."

"I'm used to it."

"From Ranger School?"

That was a topic he had no intention of discussing. "Your body needs rest to repair itself."

"I can't sleep." She shoved her fingers through her hair and shook her head. "All I can think about is Scotty. If he's okay. If he's scared. If I'll find him in time." Her hands landed back on her lap and her face turned sheepish. "Can you do that thing you did before? That Reiki?"

Why not? It would relax her. One of them should sleep. "Lie down."

He shuffled over to where she lay and offered a small prayer before he placed his hands over her eyes and the prickly warmth of Reiki energy flowed through his palms.

"I'm scared," she said. "All the time. About everything."

"No talking."

"Other than spiders, what are you afraid of?"

"I had three older brothers. The youngest of them was five years older than me. They were big and brawny and I was scrawny. While we were kids, the goal of their lives was to terrorize me."

"You're not scrawny. Not anymore."

"Doesn't mean fear goes away."

"Even now? You have to be as big as they are."

"We're good friends now. But there's always something else."

"Like Ranger School."

"Why are you stuck on that subject?"

"Because it changed you. It changed Tommy. And I don't understand why."

He was glad his hands hid the curious draw of her eyes. "Ranger School was hell. Every day I was afraid of freezing or starving or dying."

"But you made it."

"Because when I stumbled, I got up anyway." And sometimes it had felt as if every joule of energy was being sapped straight from his blood.

She was silent for a long while, and he could sense the turmoil of her ruminations.

"The scar on your palm," she said, "it matches the one on Tommy's palm."

He snapped his hands away and remembered....

"Blood brothers," Tommy said, drawing the edge of

his blade across his palm. The wall of water, veiling their hideaway, baptized their vow.

"Blood brothers," Sabriel answered, cutting his own palm, then reached for Tommy's hand. They shook, bloody palm to bloody palm, and Sabriel made a solemn promise. "I'll watch your back."

"And I'll watch yours." Tommy had laughed then. "You'll have the tougher job."

The strangled emotions of that summer when they'd both run away from pain returned, twisting through him like a heated knife. He'd never shared those feelings. He'd kept them packed away in deep parts of himself where even he couldn't find them. But there was Nora, looking at him with those wide, old-soul eyes. She understood hell.

He returned his hands to their position and relaxed until the energy flowed once more. "Tommy and I made a pact that summer. I broke that promise."

She traced the scar with the tip of her index finger, triggering a shower of sparks up his arms and a blast of need that made him want more. More contact. More sensation. More…her. He balled his hands until he had his body back under control, then placed them alongside her ears and continued with the Reiki.

"Tell me about Anna," she said.

No, he thought. Then maybe. Maybe if Nora understood his failures, she wouldn't expect so much from him. And he'd remind himself why she didn't fit into his plans.

"Anna was twenty-one when I noticed her." He gave a short, sharp laugh. The skinny, gloating duckling he'd met years before had turned into a long-legged swan. "She was working on her biology thesis. How the human body adapts to survive under extreme conditions. How men could take the mental and physical abuse of Ranger School fascinated her."

Nora snorted. "With the Colonel as her father, it's no surprise."

"The Colonel gave her access to the Ranger School recruits. Camden Laboratories had developed a drug that shut down the brain's pain center and the soldiers' need for sleep. The theory was that it would allow them to perform at higher levels long enough to complete their mission—no matter how long it took."

"The class you and Tommy were in. That was the first group to try the drug?"

"Human guinea pigs." His hands moved to the next position over the crown of her head. "We were told it was a vitamin supplement to help us get through Ranger School. At first, Anna thought what she was doing was helping people, but when she saw the results, she begged the Colonel to stop the testing." Forgetting all about Reiki, Sabriel scrubbed a hand over his face to dislodge the flashes of memories snapping through his mind.

He cleared his throat and scooped his hands under Nora's nape. The relaxation of her head in his hands unwound the tightness in his chest. "But the Colonel insisted that the project was on course and tried to hide the negatives and amp the positives. She saw how the soldiers got hurt. One died—suicide. Most had hallucinations and were left with lingering PTSD. Tommy's mind…fried."

"That wasn't her fault. Or yours."

"I was a coward." *Tell the truth about what you see and do.* Roger's Rangers Standing Order Number 4.

"You? No."

"I went against a direct order. I never took the drug. I kept quiet." Not one of the team. An outsider. Never a real Ranger, despite the tab on his uniform shoulder. "But Tommy knew."

"The choice to take the drug or not was Tommy's, not yours."

"He was sensitive to everything. Hell, he couldn't even take aspirin without his stomach bleeding. And once he started on this experimental drug, the addiction was instantaneous. He needed more and more of it to get through the grueling days."

The memory was a stone in his heart and he rubbed at the weight. "He was afraid of the Colonel. He was a Camden. He *couldn't* wash out. I'd seen how the Colonel treated him. The pressure. The expectations. I'd promised to help him through." Sabriel shook his head. "But I couldn't always pick up his slack or fix his mistakes. I let him down."

"He earned his tab. I saw it on his uniform."

Sabriel slid his hands to her shoulders. "One patrol short."

Day eleven of a twelve-day patrol. The wind whipped miserable cold into every pore. Rain made it impossible to see. They were pushed to the limits of endurance. But what snapped in Tommy wasn't physical. It was mental. "On the last day, he cracked."

And spent the next two years in a mental hospital, getting his chemistry rebalanced.

"What does the study have to do with Anna's death?"

Everything. "She thought Tommy's breakdown was her fault. She knew how much Tommy needed to succeed, for the Colonel's sake. Tommy begged for more—just to get through. And she gave him an extra dose. When he cracked, she quit her thesis, school, the lab—everything." Anna had turned to Sabriel when the Colonel had given her an ultimatum and she'd refused to go back to the research. "We got married. But the Colonel wouldn't leave her alone. He'd find a thousand little ways to let her know what a disappointment she was. She started taking more and more personal risks."

He swallowed around the knot in his throat. "She got into freediving to escape all the tension with her father."

"What's freediving?"

"Diving without an air tank." In the water, she was magical—a mermaid. She had a concentration of energy that allowed her to break barriers others only dreamed of. She was at her calmest right before a dive, going deep inside herself to make the world, the worries, disappear. All that was left, she'd once told him, was pure mind.

"She went for record after record." Always needed to go a little deeper into the quiet, into the peace. He'd hoped that this peace in the deep of the sea would save her, even if the depth of his love for her couldn't. "All to prove that she wasn't a failure."

"Like Tommy." Nora's voice was thick with tears.

Sabriel could still see the image of Anna captured by

the ESPN crew taping her record attempt on that day. The black and neon-green wet suit fitting her body like skin. Her long blond hair, a cascade of curls around her long, slim face. And that faraway look in her eyes, as if she was seeing something no one else could see.

He'd tried to tell her to forget the Colonel, to concentrate on the life they were making together, their plans for a family of their own. But something about the Camden doctrine just wouldn't let her go.

"Sometimes she had to exhaust herself swimming laps before she could sleep." But she couldn't give up. And a cloud hung over their happiness, a gnawing fear that she couldn't ever escape the expectations, the feeling of failure.

"When someone broke her record, she had to go right back out and go deeper." Sabriel moved his hands above Nora's throat, drew the symbol of power in his mind's eye and continued. "Anna was fifteen miles off the Florida coast. I was hundreds of miles away, trying to explain to a board of my peers why I'd disobeyed a direct order from a commanding officer."

"Wait for me, Anna. I'll be there tomorrow."

"There's a storm coming in," she said, and he could hear that tight despair in her voice. *"I need to get the dive in before the rain hits. The sponsors—"*

"Can damn well wait. I'm your safety diver."

"I've got a whole crew to take care of me."

"She broke her record," Sabriel said, shaking off the soap-bubble image of Anna as she walked off the boat and into the deep blue water. "But when it was time to come back up, her lift bag didn't inflate and she lost consciousness."

Time, he could still feel its maddening speed, its torturing slowness. The frenzy that had come over him at the news of her accident. His mad race to reach her.

Too far. Too late.

"By the time I got to the hospital," he said, "she was dead."

And the Colonel, seeking to hurt him, had slapped a copy of the video taken at the scene by the television crew into his hands and told him Anna's death was his fault, that he would have to pay.

Sabriel had watched the tape helplessly time and again, watched as the divers had surfaced, watched as bloody foam poured from Anna's mouth, watched her limp body being whisked away by ambulance.

He'd demanded answers. He'd inspected every frame of video, every piece of her equipment.

That's when he'd understood the truth. That she'd wanted to die. That she'd waited for the one time he couldn't save her to escape.

Everything after that was a blur. The funeral, his dishonorable discharge from the Army, the Colonel's negligence lawsuit. He couldn't eat. He couldn't sleep. He couldn't work. A hole formed inside him and nothing could sew it back together.

He'd given up on saving the world. Less toll on the heart to attack the situation from the other side—first with the U.S. Marshals, then with Seekers. Find the scum and put them where they wouldn't hurt anyone.

The one thing he knew for sure was that he couldn't lie down and die. He couldn't let the Colonel win.

Not then, not now.

IN THE DARK of this loft, in the warm nest of sleeping bag and hay, with the relaxing waves of Sabriel's magic hands still humming through her body, talking seemed natural.

"Anna's death wasn't your fault." Tenderness squeezed Nora's heart at the pain he'd had to endure. She wanted to wrap her arms around him, but sensed he wouldn't appreciate such a gesture, so she sat up and tucked her arms around her legs over the sleeping bag. "If anyone's responsible, it's the Colonel."

"Dying was the only way she could escape him. I wish—" Sabriel went back to the loft opening and studied the landscape. "It doesn't matter."

"Of course it does." The sadness etching his face against the stark light of the farmyard made her want to comfort him as he'd comforted her with his hands. She hugged her knees tighter. "Loving someone, losing them, it's always hard, no matter what."

Sabriel's frankness about Anna was disarming, demanding an equal measure of truth. She couldn't ease his sorrow, but she could share her failures, the ones she'd never dared speak for fear they would taint her.

"I met Tommy when he called my midnight-to-four-a.m. show. *Nora at Night*—I know, not very original, but it was my boss's idea. And since I was living in the basement, and he didn't know it, I wasn't about to argue."

Nora picked at the loose hay scattered on her sleeping

bag. "Tommy liked the eclectic mix of my playlists—and had called to offer suggestions of his own."

Sabriel gave a low chuckle. "Tommy and his music. Sometimes I think he used it to drown out the Colonel's voice in his head."

"He sure knew a lot—not just about the music, but about the artists, too. We talked for hours." In the cocoon of that darkness, broken spirit reached out to broken spirit. Until, months later, she'd had the courage to meet him in public and had fallen for his sweet smile almost immediately.

"I married Tommy because he made me laugh. He made me feel safe." She brushed away the loose hay in her hair, but she couldn't as easily brush away the feeling of Tommy's betrayal. "But that was Tommy on his meds. Tommy off his meds was a nightmare. And when the Colonel forced him—us—to go live at the estate, he was a completely different man."

"What happened?"

Sabriel focused on her so completely, she could not hold the intensity of his gaze.

She shrugged. "The Colonel wanted an heir, and the Colonel manipulated Tommy to get his way. I wasn't ready. Not with the way things were. Not when it felt as if we were living on top of a powder keg about to blow. But, like Anna, Tommy wanted so badly to please his father that he tampered with my birth control pills."

Sabriel swore softly, and knowing someone else was outraged at Tommy's behavior, propped her courage.

"The trust was gone and it killed our marriage." Nora

twisted a piece of hay round and round until it snapped. "After Scotty was born, I couldn't do anything right. The Colonel tried to interfere with my raising of Scotty. My breast milk wasn't good enough for a Camden. A Camden needed fortified formula. I went to Scotty too quickly when he cried. I held him too much. I played with him too much."

She'd cried so many tears that first year, enough to flood the Flint River. "I wanted to leave, but the Colonel made it clear that if I did, it was alone. Scotty was his."

"You're the mother. The laws are in your favor."

"But he's got the influence. He'd line up a dozen character witnesses who'd swear I was a bad mother." She snorted. "He used Scotty as a bartering tool. Tommy realized there was no way he could ever please his father and, in the end, he left so I could stay with Scotty."

Which had turned out to be the best thing for Tommy. "Tommy found his niche as an outdoor guide. And I really thought he'd finally found a way to be happy."

"You couldn't save him. He was already too far gone." Sabriel's words soothed her as his magic hands had earlier.

"I gave up on Tommy." And paid a price. She wasn't going to repeat her mistake. "I'm not going to give up on saving Scotty."

BEFORE DAWN, as he'd programmed himself to, Sabriel awakened. His body lay spooned against a woman's. Blessedly warm and soft. One hand rested casually on birdlike ribs, his thumb snug against the delicious curve of a breast, his nose buried in a cloud of silky hair. He burrowed closer, a hum of contentment purring all the way down to his marrow.

For an instant, memories of Anna sprang to mind. A rush of pure need made him rock hard. Until the scent of sweet almonds and hay reached his brain.

Hell, not Anna, but Nora. In old man Wagner's hay loft. A woman who'd already had a lifetime of betrayals and didn't need another from a man with no heart.

Cautiously, he pulled his hand from her ribs. She mumbled something in her sleep, folded his hand into both of hers and settled deeper into the *V* of his body, intensifying his hunger for her.

Acutely conscious of the soft texture of her skin, the way her curves fit so nicely to his body, the innocent trust lining her face, he sought to free his hand one more time without waking her up. And almost made it before her eyes sprang open and pure fear widened them until they all but swallowed her face.

"Shh," he said, ignoring the compromising position of his body. "We have to leave. Before the old man gets up."

Nodding, she scampered out of her sleeping bag and silently helped him pack.

Sabriel copped half a dozen eggs from the still sleeping hens and left a couple dollar bills in the eggs' place. He grinned at the thought of old Mr. Wagner's surprise when he reached under the hen and came up with a dollar instead of an egg.

Once in the woods again, he hard-boiled his loot in the Jetboil and insisted Nora eat a couple, as well as one of his homemade energy bars before they continued. Today's hike would be no picnic; they needed all the fuel they could get.

They skirted the bog and made it to the other side of the meadow, then plunged into the woods once again. Dawn burst in an explosion of red against a clear sky. But the sunshine wouldn't last. The smell of rain rode on the breeze and the changing atmospheric pressure squeezed at his sinus cavity.

He glommed on to the trail left by their hunters.

"That doesn't look like Tommy's and Scotty's tracks," Nora said behind him.

She was learning fast. "Nope."

"Then why are we following them?"

"Know thine enemy."

Chapter Nine

"Know your enemy?" Nora asked, pushing herself faster to keep up with Sabriel. Trees blurred in her peripheral vision. The rocky, rooty ground demanded concentration. Dawn's chill was gone and sweat from the fast pace already soaked her back. She should take off a layer, but she didn't want to get left behind. "We already know them. They belong to the Colonel. They want us to have an accident. They want Scotty."

"We don't know how many there are," Sabriel said, the voice of calm to her tangled web of anxiety. "The degree of their training. What equipment they're carrying. The state of their morale."

"We can't follow the men hunting us. That's plain insanity. They'll get ahead. They'll get to Scotty first."

Sabriel was a bloodhound on a scent, and nothing she said was getting through.

"You can get to know a man better through his tracks than by seeing him," he said. "If we know them, we can beat them."

"Or they can stop us. Kill us. Take Scotty back to the Colonel. Do you want him to crack and break the way Tommy did? The way Anna did?"

Sabriel slanted her a look over his shoulder and his eyes glittered ice-cold.

Stop it! Stop manipulating with guilt the way the Colonel does. It makes you no better than he is. "I'm sorry, I—"

"You're going to give up?"

Her hands fisted. "No, never!"

"I've taken you this far." His expression focused and intent, he zeroed in on the tracks and plunged down the side of a ravine. She had no choice. She had to follow.

Trust. She had to trust that little voice inside that told her he was an honorable man. But none of what he did made sense. His actions seemed to drag her down into a deeper hell.

"Footprints indicate six men," Sabriel said, interrupting the dark tangle of her thoughts as he crossed over a brook.

She sucked in a breath. "Six? That many?"

"They're traveling light, and they're getting hungry."

"You can't possibly tell that from a track."

"What you think and what you feel shows up in the pressure releases. Tracks are like windows into a person's soul." He continued stalking, studying the tracks, taking them up a gradual climb. "They're trained, but cocky. They *know* they're going to win. They're following Tommy's tracks decently enough—but then Tommy can't really hide his tracks because of Scotty." Sabriel pointed to a scratch on a beech. "Waist-high scuff on this tree shows they're armed. One of them has a rifle."

"What difference does it make if one of them has a rifle? They've got guns and they plan to kill us."

"A rifle gives them range. But the hunted has the advantage. These hunters aren't part of the wilderness. They're just trespassing aliens."

She snorted. "Too bad their mother ship isn't calling them home."

Half his mouth quirked up. "Maybe we can make them think she is."

She frowned. "What exactly are you planning to do?"

"Even the odds."

Another one of his take-charge phrases that pushed her out. *Don't worry your pretty little head over this.* How many times had she heard the Colonel say those words to his wife? How many times had he used a not-so-polite version on her? "You have to stop treating me like a brainless twit."

"It'll buy us time."

"Hey!" She grabbed his elbow and yanked. "I'm not the one who's ten."

He turned around, a flash of hurt hardening his eyes. "Will you trust me, Nora?"

"Only if you trust me."

"Fair enough." He turned back to tracking. "I'm going to try to get close enough to see what we're up against."

"Then?"

"I won't know until I see."

Not very comforting, but his job wasn't to comfort

her, and she'd asked for straight talk. She hated to divert even one minute from the path that would take her to Scotty, but Sabriel was her guide and she needed him. She would give him the slack he asked for if it bought them time.

The pitter-patter of rain started soon after lunch, the striking sound of it more a nuisance than the widely spaced drops. After a short pause to wolf down a pouch of tuna and some fruit leather, and to change socks, they were on their way again, following the endless trail of tracks that seemed to lead nowhere.

After the rain, came the sun, taking the chill out of the air, making the afternoon warm enough to strip down to the base shirt layer.

Sabriel pointed out the single thread dangling from a branch. "See where this branch snapped? One of them plowed through here. Look at the break."

"It looks fresh."

He nodded, pleased, and his pleasure fluttered inside her. "They're not far ahead."

"Whatever you do, it can't hurt our chances of finding Scotty."

"There's always a risk, Nora, that's part of living."

She walked in helpless frustration, wishing she could do more to help her son.

The closer they got to the Colonel's men, the more Sabriel morphed into a predator on a hunt, bent over, his footsteps higher, faster, quieter than before. The more he became one with the forest, the more she felt like an alien who'd landed on the wrong planet—ugly, clumsy, plodding. The dimming afternoon light didn't help the feeling.

She gave a silent snort. Until she'd had Scotty, her worst fear had been to be left alone on a street corner. After Scotty, her fears had transferred to all the things that could harm him. But in all of her worst nightmares, she'd never pictured herself running in the woods with her son's life on the line. She'd never pictured being chased, her own life in danger.

Sabriel slowed and pointed out shuffle marks. "Shows they stopped here and looked behind."

"For us?"

He shrugged. "Maybe they just liked the view."

Or maybe they were on to Sabriel's ruse and were setting a trap for them. The thorniest part of their two-part mission executed, they could nab Scotty. Catching him was just a matter of miles.

Afternoon light snuffed out early in the mountains, bleeding the sky in a canvas of bloody red before dropping behind the mountaintops. Sabriel's pace slowed, his footsteps became more measured—a fox scenting a chicken coop. He stopped at the base of a steep incline. One finger traced the faintly discolored stones turned over by passing feet, revealing their darker underside. "They've holed up on the ridge to rest for the night."

She could barely make out his voice. "Then we should leave," she said, with equal care. "Get ahead. We've already wasted most of a day." He'd promised her she'd find Scotty today, that she'd hold her son in her arms. Instead they'd followed the Colonel's men on a useless chase, let Scotty get farther away.

"We're going to do the unexpected," Sabriel whispered, retracing his steps. "It's our best chance to even the odds."

"This isn't the time to play macho games."

"It's going to buy us time. Divide and conquer."

"We're not at war."

"Of course we are. The prize is your son."

The gut punch of truth had her hand clamping over her heaving stomach. Her voice was a thread she fought to keep from breaking. "How will whatever you're going to do help us find Scotty?"

"Without food and weapons, they won't be as much of a threat."

She shook her head, the weight of terror sinking to her feet. "What if you get caught? How will I find him?"

"I've never been seen."

"There's always a first time."

"Give me an inch, Nora. I'll get you the prize."

That huge a slice of trust was too much to ask when Scotty's life was on the line. Truth was, she couldn't bear to see Sabriel hurt, either. The Colonel's men had orders. They always followed orders. A shudder raced down her spine. And in this wilderness, making a body, or two or three, disappear was too easy.

Sabriel wound around the mountain until he reached a thick tangle of bushes from where he could observe the thugs' camp. Close enough to hear their too-loud voices. Close enough that, if they were spotted, Boggs's rifle could easily pick them off. Sabriel was right. The type of weapon did make a difference. Worry descended on her in a cloak of lead.

Sabriel retreated deeper into the woods, to a safe distance away from the camp. He handed her an energy bar, ordered her to eat, then applied camouflage right over his clothes, using the mud, dirt and soil of the land, sculpting himself into a shadow of texture and color that made him virtually invisible against the forest.

She watched Sabriel prepare for warfare and the almonds and apricots of the energy bar turned into a tasteless paste that scratched her dry throat. He'd stripped every sign of civilization from his body, leaving only a savage essence. He bore the total transformation as magnificently as the tuxedo he'd worn on her wedding day.

His green eyes, when they met hers, burned with a fierceness of purpose that made her want to dab on mud, and shed the scared mouse trembling inside her—transform herself into a confident warrior able to face the Colonel, tell him exactly what she thought of the way he handled people.

Sabriel had faced the Colonel, and Sabriel had won. That gave her hope for herself and for Scotty. They could escape. They could have a life outside the estate.

"You okay?" Sabriel asked.

Unable to trust her voice, she nodded and put away the second half of the energy bar in her jacket pocket. She'd played a part for so long now that she wasn't sure who the real Nora was anymore. The one thing she did know was that she couldn't go on like this, scared, always scared. Not if she was going to hang on to Scotty.

Sabriel shifted fallen branches to form a thicker shield around her. "Tommy's last sign said he was going to Blueberry Hill."

She was in no mood for Tommy's wordplay right now. He'd gotten her into this mess. He was the one risking Scotty's life because of whatever harebrained notion he'd gotten stuck into his sick mind. "Yeah, what a thrill."

"What's your problem?"

Because she wanted to hit something, anything and he was standing there next to her, she stuffed her hands under her armpits. "I'm just mad. Mad at Tommy for taking Scotty. Mad that I can't help you. Mad at myself for not fighting to get away earlier and avoiding this whole situation."

"The Colonel's good at finding a man's weakness and using it against him. He used Scotty to control you."

"Doesn't make rolling over any more pleasant."

"No, it doesn't. But trust me when I say, you've survived longer than a lot of men."

The breeze surfed through the trees, whispering the words neither of them could say. *Longer than Tommy. Longer than Anna.*

Sabriel stepped behind Nora and turned her around. Arm extended over her shoulder, he pointed at the horizon. "See that knob over there? The patch of short shrubs?"

Even caked in mud, there was a confident solidness to him, to his body, one that went straight to her gut. She nodded.

"That's what we called Blueberry Hill, because of the

lowbush blueberries that grow there. Tommy's next sign will be there."

"Why are you telling me this? You said you never got caught. You said—"

"A Ranger is always ready for unexpected trouble." He unbuckled the holster from his hip, then slipped out the weapon and stood next to her, showing her how to operate it. "If you have to use this, aim for the biggest part of the target and shoot."

Her hands flew up and her voice came out in a low, guttural growl. "I can't use a gun!"

"Not even to protect your son?"

She relented. Her hands fell to her sides and turned over, palms up, to accept his offering. For Scotty, she'd do anything. She'd die. She'd kill. "What about you?"

"It'll get in the way."

Signs. She'd been good at interpreting them as a kid, taking her mother's little presents, guessing what each meant. She closed her eyes and shook her head to banish the vignette of images flaring up against her will. An ice-cream cone or a chocolate bar—her mother would have a "friend" over and need quiet time. A Happy Meal—Mom would be gone late into the night, maybe even until morning. A brand-new Walkman, and Nora had known those taillights would never turn around.

A gun. He was giving her a gun.

"You had better come back," she snarled, fingernails biting into the cold steel of the pistol. How had she let this happen? How had she become so dependent on him?

He leaned forward and pecked her cheek, branding her with the still damp mud of his disguise.

She slapped a hand over her cheek, feeling it warm. "What was that for?"

"Stay right here. You'll be safe. Remember the birdcall?"

She nodded.

"If you hear anyone else approaching, be ready to shoot. I'll be back in four hours." He turned to leave.

So long? She grabbed his wrist.

He smiled. "Ah, you like me. You really like me."

"You're such a jerk." Her grip relaxed. "Four hours."

"It's a date."

SABRIEL HAD TOLD HER to stay put, but she couldn't sit, curled into a ball, her imagination magnifying every noise, every eternal second into a disaster. She dug the palm-size binoculars she'd seen Sabriel use from the pack he'd left behind and one slow step at a time made her way back to the edge of the brush about two hundred feet from the camp. On her stomach, she wedged in until she had a good view, but was still hidden.

The men sat in a loose circle. Their attention wasn't on their surroundings, but on their meal. No one stood sentinel. No one guarded their flank. Wasn't that a basic? But then why should they care? They were hunters. And they thought their prey was running scared.

That's how she'd been, too, living with blinders, seeing only what she needed to see to survive. The roof over her head. The three squares. The financial support. Except that the roof might as well have been supported by bars. She could never eat what she wanted, only what was placed in front of her. She might not have had a mortgage to pay, but she also hadn't handled more than spare change in over ten years. What was so grown-up about depending on someone else for everything?

She caught a glimpse of Sabriel. He blended with the trees, became a bush, hid behind a stump. A shadow, he moved to the far edge of the camp, unseen by the men whose goal was to capture him—or at least stop him with a bullet.

One man against six. Armed men. And the arrogant fool had gone to them without his gun—only a knife and some rope. Her lips rolled in and her teeth sealed them shut.

Please, please make him come back safely.

Scotty needed him. She needed him. If he got in trouble, was she close enough to hit a target? Did she have the courage to squeeze the trigger? She pulled the weapon from the holster and placed it within reach.

Through the binoculars, she watched as Costlow got up and stretched. Everything about him was square, from his head to his torso to his hands. The overall effect reminded her of the Lego robots Scotty still liked to build on rainy afternoons. Costlow walked away from the group—right toward the last spot Nora had seen Sabriel. She sucked in her breath, held it trapped. Costlow unzipped his fly and let out a stream of urine.

She jammed a hand over her mouth. She wanted to scream, run, laugh, cry all at the same time. Sabriel was going to get caught. He was going to leave her stranded and her beautiful boy would end up another one of the Colonel's failed experiments. What was she supposed to do? Just sit there and watch him die?

Give him a chance, Nora. He knows what he's doing. She raised the binoculars to her eyes and focused on the group.

Where was Sabriel? As hard as she tried, she couldn't see him.

The men began to turn in, using their packs as pillows. Soon they shuffled, snuffled and eventually snored. Sabriel made no sound as he flowed through the camp so slowly she could barely see him, even when she cranked up the power on the binoculars. He planted Boggs's knife on the man next to him, switched some of the contents of one pack to another's, placed the socks—drying on a bush—in the coffeepot. Moving as if in slow motion, he plucked a weapon here, another there. He took the MREs remaining in the men's packs and stuffed them down his shirt, then disappeared.

A stone landed on the man closest to the brush. Frowning, the man sat up and looked around. He seemed to listen to something coming from behind him. The man reached for his pistol and headed into the brush.

A wave of sick fear surged over her. Should she cause some sort of distraction, draw the man away from Sabriel so he could escape? She was too far to shoot or throw rocks. And either of those options would wake up the rest of the camp. And if the Colonel's men got her, they got Scotty. But she couldn't let Sabriel die, either. She'd never wanted to put anyone—him—in danger.

She had to get closer.

EVERYTHING AROUND Sabriel slowed, became in tune with the rhythm of the earth. No tension, no nerves, no anything, except awareness—of every breath, of every heartbeat, of every ripple in the invisible field that moved through all things. The preparations were done. All he needed was to tug the right string to set his mission in motion.

He lured the man on the outskirt of the camp out of sleep with a rock and the tantalizing sounds of a footstep or two. Weapon drawn, the soldier slipped into the brush and into the woods.

Just as if he'd been coached, he followed the path Sabriel had laid to the narrow ravine, and hit the trigger Sabriel had set. The spike from the trap whipped through the air, catching him right below the knee in a powerful wallop. The man rolled on the ground holding his knee in agony. Before he recovered, Sabriel had him gagged and trussed like a Thanksgiving turkey. The small cave would hold him until he could ensnare the others. Someone would have to know where to look to see him in the thick brush at the bottom of the ravine.

The next man stepped into a pit trap, spraining his ankle. Sabriel tied him near the first man, lashing one to the other.

The third backed into a leg-hold trap and Sabriel added another token to his bad-guy chain.

Three more to go, and he and Nora would have a clear trail to Scotty.

Adrenaline revved from the successful hunt, Sabriel approached the camp once again and two things hit him at once: Nora had moved from her safe position and Boggs's satellite phone was ringing.

Swearing silently, he retreated and made his way around the camp. He'd only gotten four sidearms and Boggs's rifle. Boggs and Hutt still had their pistols.

Nora moved again. His heart knocked. What was she doing? If she took another step, Boggs would see her. Didn't she realize she was putting herself in danger?

Moving faster than he liked and risking discovery, he reached her, clamped a hand over her mouth and pulled her back into the brush.

"What are you doing?" he growled.

She gasped and rolled over on her back, ready to kick and fight. "Saving you."

He closed his eyes and shook his head. Saving him. The little fool. "Next time, wait. You almost got us caught. I had to leave two pistols and three men behind."

"I—" she started, then blinked as if she were holding back tears. "I'm sorry. I thought they'd found you."

"And what were you planning to do?"

"You told me to aim for the biggest target."

Things were getting messy. When he called Seekers for the pickup of the Colonel's men, he should leave her behind. He could get to Scotty faster without her, keep her safer in Seekers' care. He helped her up. "Let's roll before the rest of them wake up and all hell breaks loose."

With a nod, she followed him back to where they'd left the packs.

"How did you know they wouldn't see you?" she asked.

"Practice. Tommy and I used to play this game all the time, leaving people scratching their heads. The only rule was that no one get hurt by our pranks."

"But I could see you."

Sabriel reached around to help her down a tricky stack of rocks. "You knew what to look for. The Colonel's men were too intent on their own agendas to think that we might backtrack and take a look at what was going on right where they were."

"But Boggs. He looked right at you."

"He saw what he expected to see—tree trunks. All I had to do was find the hole in his awareness." He cocked his head, listened to the broken surf of wind.

"Where the hell are Garo and Aggas? Hilferty?" Boggs's shout cut the night air. "What do you mean they're missing?"

Behind them, the tempest of chaos erupted.

Chapter Ten

The echo of chaos fell away as Sabriel led Nora over the next crest of mountain. The moon played peekaboo with scalloped clouds. Amazing how many stars freckled the navy skin of sky. Thing was, she shouldn't have time to notice these things. Even though her footing was shaky in the darkness, they should be walking faster while they had the chance to get ahead.

At the rate they were moving, they'd never catch up to Tommy and Scotty, and the Colonel's men would round them up as easily as cattle.

"I can walk faster, you know," Nora said, unable to keep her irritation from boiling over.

"I know, my super woman. I'm making sure we have enough gas to go the distance."

Damn him, he was laughing at her. And his slow pace was having another unnerving effect. With night cloaking the woods that usually distracted her, she was aware of him. Of his constant proximity. The steady, calm of his voice. The brush of his fingers against hers when he passed her an energy bar or offered her some trail mix. Of the strength of his hand on her shoulder when he asked her how she was holding up. A simple gesture that left her so flushed, she had to take off an extra layer to dissipate its heat.

"We're going to have to rest soon." Sabriel stopped and reached for his hydration tube.

Nora pressed by him only to realize she had no idea where he was heading. "We have to keep going."

"You're dead on your feet."

"Super women can keep going when their kid's in danger."

"Even super women have to change their socks."

She wanted to spit out more of the venom poisoning her thoughts, but he was right again. Her feet were getting too hot and blisters would not help her keep up the pace. She sat on a fallen log and dug out a pair of dry, if not clean, socks and unlaced her boots.

And as much as she counted on his strength, his skill, his confidence to get her to Scotty, she had to learn to take charge of her own fate. She had to make sure that she could find her way to Scotty and back to civilization. "Show me how to find my way in the woods."

The moonlight's shadows hid his expression, but could not disguise the intentness of his study. "I'll take you where you need to go."

Now she'd gone and hurt his feelings. "I'm not doubting your ability. But if something happens to you, I have to be able to get help." She hung her damp socks on her pack, avoiding the piercing prod of his gaze.

"Your cell phone hasn't worked in days. Not that I could tell anyone where to find us."

He sat in silence, unlacing his boots, changing his socks, then retying the laces with meticulous care. "At the next stream," he said, "we'll stop and, while the filter purifies water for our hydration bags, I'll show you the basics of map and compass."

"Deal." Her lungs emptied on one long release of air, unpenning tension and giving her steps a new bounce.

The next stream took an hour to find. Already, the purple break of dawn rimmed the peaks of mountains. Fatigue ached through her body, making her bones and muscles heavy and her eyes gritty. "What can I do while you purify the water?"

"Get out the Jetboil and some oatmeal. Grab the map and compass while you're at it."

He washed the mud of his camouflage from his face and hands. Then, while he pumped water, he explained the marking on the map—how contour lines worked, where they were now, and Tommy's two possible destinations, the hiking trails, the highways, the rivers, what the colors meant, and the easiest way to find help.

"But Tommy isn't using a regular map," Sabriel said, taking a break from pumping water to start the stove.

Nora sat back on her heels and wrapped her arms around her knees. "What kind of map, then?"

"Songlines."

She frowned. "Songlines?"

"It's an ancient navigational system used by aboriginal people. It creates invisible footpaths across the land.

Cues that act like road signs even in a place like this forest where one hill pretty much looks like the next and one creek is hard to tell from another."

"How?"

"Look back. Remember how we talked about birches and how they tend to die young?"

She nodded, seeing the trio of white birches at the top of the hill in the graying light of dawn, remembering the shredded state of their papery bark.

"If I took you there and asked you to think about the last conversation we had, you could probably find the point and retrace your steps to it." He smiled as he capped the hydration bag and slid it back in her pack. "Tommy, though, he started giving the reference points song titles and then he'd sing them all together to make himself a map. Off-key. You know how he can't carry a tune to save his life. Since I hung out with him, I got caught up in the game, too."

"'Route 66,' 'Farmer in the Dell,' 'Blueberry Hill,'" Nora whispered, a new respect forming for Tommy's outside-the-box brain.

The thought of songlines appealed to her. Songs, stacking them up into playlists, their beats, their lyrics, their emotions had allowed her to survive her mother's rocky romances—their lustful beginnings, their stormy middles, their bitter endings. George had been the exception. His arrival and his departure had both been quiet. Not her mother's style at all. Maybe that's why Nora had liked him so much. George had given her her first radio for her eleventh birthday. She'd learned to tune out her mother's drama, and tune in the radio to blissful escape.

"You know Tommy's songline," she said and looked up at Sabriel with renewed admiration. "That's why you don't need the map. That's how you know he's going to either Mount Storm or Goose Neck Mountain."

"Pilgrim's Peak is in the other direction."

"Teach me his song."

Sabriel ate up the last of his oatmeal with more gusto than warranted. "I told you I'd get you and your son back safely."

"Like you said," Nora said, washing up her oatmeal-gummed cup, "it doesn't hurt to be ready for unexpected trouble."

So he gave her Tommy's song and, with each title, hope of soon holding her son burgeoned. *I'm coming for you, Scotty.*

THE TRAIN TRESTLE joined the Kestrel and Merlin campgrounds. The nineteen-mile triangle of tracks was on a pocket of privately owned land that bordered the Gray Goose Wilderness Area and was maintained for the use of an old-fashioned steam engine that pulled three dining cars, a four-star kitchen and a glass observation car that made the riders feel as if they were flying over the valley. On the two-hour ride, passengers were served a four-course meal and breathless views.

Technically, he and Nora were trespassing. Not that anyone policed the tracks so high off the ground. Not that they had any choice with the Colonel's men closing in on them. Nora had fallen asleep sitting up, repeating Tommy's songline over and over again. She'd been on her feet for almost a day. He'd figured he could give her an hour. What he hadn't figured was that the Colonel's men would catch up to them so fast.

The train tracks were the shortest way to get across the mile-wide gorge and to a phone to get help with his cell dead. "Come on."

Nora stayed planted on the legal side of the tracks, eyeing them as if they were vipers that would rear back and bite. "Those are train tracks."

"You're a sharp observer, super woman."

She frowned at him. "There could be a train."

"Closed for the season." Though he wasn't sure.

She tentatively stepped onto the tracks, shaking as she looked over the side at the rusty-looking structure holding them five stories above the ground and the tiny line of a creek meandering below.

"Don't look down and you'll be fine."

"Sure. I can do this."

Going over the schedule in his mind, Nora following him, he stepped from tie to tie with confident strides. One lunch service. One dinner service. April to October. But just when in October the train stopped running, he couldn't remember.

They were halfway across the gorge when a deep-throated roll, long and drawn out, reverberated in the air. Hell, he'd guessed wrong. They couldn't race fast enough to beat the train back to far side of the gorge. Not that the business end of Boggs's pistol was a destination of choice. That left forward, head-on, until the next support tower.

"That's a train whistle." Nora stumbled over a tie. His hand twisted back to steady her, then tugged to prod her along.

"Yep." He kept running, holding her hand tight in his, keeping her ahead of her fears.

"It's coming closer."

"Yep."

"There's no ground next to the track in case you hadn't noticed," she said, voice not quite steady. "We're stranded in midair."

"Yep."

The silver nose of the engine rounded the mountain's flank, came straight at them.

"Sabriel!"

"Come on, Nora. Don't quit on me now."

"We're going to die!"

"Not today."

The click-clack of wheels raced with his thoughts. Gauging the architecture below him from the shadows slanting onto the trees, he stopped and turned to face her. "Climb over."

Her chest pumped air in and out of her overworked lungs. Her eyes took over her face. "Over where?"

"The side. There's a support right under you."

Her mouth dropped open. "You want me to—"

"You want to argue or you want to stay in one piece?" The beastly shape of the train rammed toward them in a clatter of iron on iron, its long, deep whistle, a deafening warning. Sabriel shinnied down the side, braced himself on the iron lacework and reached for Nora.

She muttered something he couldn't make out, but got down on her knees and slinked down the side, inch by careful inch, shaking all the way, but moving. The girl was tough.

"I've got you." He guided her feet onto the iron brace. "Slide down."

She did, ending up snug in the *V* of the narrow brace.

The train chugged above them, click-clacking against the rails, right into their bones, threatening to jolt them right off their perch. Its whistle rent the crisp autumn air, echoing eerily against the mountains surrounding the valley in a crown, piercing brain, shocking heart. Sandwiched between his body and the support, Nora had nowhere to go, but he tightened his grip anyway and firmly chased away the image of her plunging down into the abyss below.

"I've got you," he said into her ear. "I won't let you fall."

"If you do," she answered back, "I'll kill you."

He laughed. "That's my girl."

Resolve under stress. Pulling up her bootstraps even though she was scared spitless and keeping her goal foremost in her mind. With her for a mother, Scotty had a chance of surviving the Colonel's soul-stealing influence.

Because Sabriel couldn't help himself, he stroked her hair, his gaze never leaving hers until the throb of train on track ebbed and the whistle gave one last mournful wail.

"You okay?" he asked, and pushed away from the soft curves of her body.

She nodded, then jabbed him in the chest with the heel of her hand. "Done for the season?"

"Slight miscalculation." That could have had dire results.

"You almost got us killed."

Almost lost her Scotty. Almost handed the Colonel another victory. Having seen the Colonel's work at close range, Sabriel understood her fear.

Movement on the far side of the tracks caught his attention. The Colonel's men. Three of them, curbed for now three-quarters of a mile away, by the train chugging toward them. "We're going to have company as soon as the train rounds the bend. Let's roll."

He helped her back up onto the tracks, and they ran the quarter mile to the other side of the gorge. On solid ground once more, they paralleled the tracks to the station where Sabriel knew there was a pay phone.

He scanned the station, empty now that the train held the squirm of passengers captive, found no signs that Boggs had called ahead to have someone waiting to pick them up. "I need to make a phone call."

Still holding his hand, Nora balked. "We can't go there. The Colonel's men are going to find us. We have to keep going."

Sabriel wasn't an impulsive man. Work was done in calculated steps. He erred on the side of caution, his taste for adrenaline having died a long time ago. He wasn't given to sentiment. Ranger School had taught him that the best of plans could sometimes go awry and that a soldier had to be prepared for unforeseen troubles. That a man had to take responsibility for his actions.

And that sometimes, the right action was asking for help.

"Can't get cell reception in this notch," he said as he stepped onto the gravel parking lot. "I've got three men tied up. This might be my only chance to call Seekers and have them picked up."

His last chance to let someone know how deep a hole he'd dug.

THE HARD RINGS of the target Nora imagined painted on the middle of her back rankled as they ran toward the station. Any second, she expected the real slam of a bullet to find the bull's-eye.

The Colonel's men had to be sprinting down the tracks by now. How long before they caught up with them? Ten minutes? Five? How could Sabriel expose them to capture when they should be widening the distance while they could?

"News flash," she said. "There's still three of the Colonel's men right behind us, and they don't want to make nice. Especially not after the mind games you played on them."

Sabriel leaped onto the platform, his hiking boots drumming a confident tune against the wood planks.

"Hello," an old man dressed like a stationmaster straight out of a history book said. The man studied them and kept struggling with the lock to the station's door. Gray hair poked from beneath his black cap and smile lines crinkled his sparkling blue eyes. "The train's already left."

"Ran into a bit of trouble," Sabriel said with a genial smile as he shook his head and looked down at his muddy clothes. "Got a phone around here? Can't get reception on my cell."

"Part of the backcountry charm." The man's smile raised the broom of his mustache to sweep his ears. "Old-fashioned rotary dial phone's around the corner."

Out of the old man's earshot, Sabriel fed quarters into the pay phone. Nora's gaze kept sweeping the tracks. On the seventh pass, she caught movement along the right side. Oh, God, was that them? Her fingers pulled nervously at the straps of her backpack.

"Hurry! They're here," she said, her voice rough from the dryness of her throat. "I can see them coming."

"I need a minute," he said.

Standing beside him, her shoulders winged, shrinking her. What price had she paid by playing along and not rocking the boat? Were the last ten years worth it if she couldn't rescue Scotty? A wave of panic had her turning to Sabriel, her hand reaching for his solid body.

Listening to whoever was on the other end of the line, his gaze rose to meet hers, and he touched her, just a brush of fingers on hers, that for a moment calmed the unrest percolating up and down her spine.

The sound of boots on gravel swept away the calm. "Sabriel."

He hung up. "Let's go."

Angling away to use the shelter of the station for as long as possible, he led her toward the woods.

He would protect her from the Colonel's men as long as they were in these mountains. He would lie for her. He would take her to her son, and he would scoop him away from the Colonel.

But what happened after? After Sabriel, his debt to Tommy paid, returned to his life? After she had Scotty safe in her arms?

Boggs spotted them and shouted.

Though Sabriel plunged her into the thick trees, nothing could erase the sensation of those hard rings on that imaginary target painted in the middle of her back.

THE COLONEL'S MEN had forced him away from his planned route. But if he headed to Blood Falls he would have several options to deceive and evade before he reached Tommy's next sign at the more secluded smaller Toby Falls half a mile away. Then back on track to trail Tommy and Scotty.

That Blood Falls tended to buzz with hikers was another plus. Their tracks would be lost among the dozens already there, giving them a chance to confuse the Colonel's men.

They jogged down the trail past a fawn pool, over smooth slabs along a tributary stream, then up the steeper incline that sported mainly beech, birch and maple trees.

The roar of the falls reached them long before they crossed the footbridge over the Blood River and got their first glimpse of them.

"Wow," Nora said, in a burst of machine-gun breath, taking in the whole of the spectacle.

Behind them came a shout. Hutt, his thin face twisted in a scream of revenge.

Sabriel swore. They couldn't outrun. They'd have to outwit. If he could maneuver fast enough, they could hide on the ledge where he and Tommy had made their blood-brother vow.

A whizzing sound flew over their heads. A flare catapulted through the air, then another, and another. They landed on the brittle needles of the hemlocks all around them, setting them crackling into a fast-moving fire.

Chapter Eleven

Nora's breath struggled to catch up with her body's need for oxygen as Sabriel hopscotched over rocks to cross the river, where no other hiker ventured. She dogged his steps, hoping she didn't slip and end up taking a swim.

Ahead, the rush of falling water tumbled over an impressive sheer of reddish-brown granite that towered as high as a city skyscraper. Thousands of gallons of water pulsed through cracks and over ledges in the bedrock and roared into a fall pool that foamed and frothed, bloodred in the late afternoon light, then raced down a series of ledges in a shock that promised to thrash and trounce.

Behind them the ravenous rush of fire rolled down the gorge, chasing them.

"Come on, Nora." Sabriel scrambled up along a steep rise of hemlocks and birches that tightly wove along the side of the water, climbing until it seemed he would start up the vertical wall of rock. They were going to get roasted alive if they stayed in the trees.

Driven by the flames and the shouts of the men

behind them, she pushed to keep up, staying on Sabriel's heels. Smoke thickened, made breathing difficult—like one of Scotty's asthma attacks. She swallowed back the flash of panic.

Partway up the trailless rise, Sabriel veered left and disappeared into the water. Reaching out from his watery perch, he pulled her into a dimple in the rock that perfectly sheltered their two bodies. Gasping, she fell into his arms.

"You're okay," he shouted above the roar of water. "We'll just stand here while the fire burns itself out."

Her thigh muscles shook from the effort of the climb and from trying to stand still on this slippery spit of rock. *You're not going to fall. You're not going to fall.*

Oh, God, her feet were right on the edge and fire was climbing right after them. She was going to fall. The water sprayed her jacket, her hair, her face. She was going to lose her shaky balance, pitch into that boiling roil and die. Or fry in the fire.

Shut up, shut up, shut up. Falling wasn't an option. Frying wasn't an option. Scotty needed her. *Hang on. You have to hang on.* Her grip on Sabriel's wrists stiffened.

"Okay." She gulped in air, forcing her pulse to slow and settle. "That was close."

Too close. Sabriel's psychological warfare on the Colonel's men hadn't shredded their alliance, it had made them only more determined to finish their mission. Kill her. Kill Sabriel. Capture Scotty and turn him over to the Colonel's cruel hand.

"They won't think to look up," Sabriel said. "People rarely do. And the fire will hide our tracks."

In spite of her clawing hold, he reached to the buckle holding her pack to her body and snapped it open.

"What are you doing?" A note of panic sharpened her voice.

"In case you fall." He jerked his chin to his own loosened buckle. "You don't want the weight of the pack to drown you."

She gulped. Great. Like she needed that image in her head right now.

A smile lightened the grim set of his face as he looked into her eyes. "Water only melts wicked witches."

A warm glow settled in her solar plexus as she hung on to his wrists with frozen fingers. The slant of sun hit the throbbing mist, shimmering something between them. "I can be wicked."

"Oh, yeah?" He dipped his head and kissed her gently, so gently, and that gentleness in the roar from the water, eroded at the terror eating her alive. Her hands slid up his arms around his neck, anchored there to hold him close. The kiss settled and her mind spun, dizzy with reasons and logic as to why she should pull back. But she couldn't find a single word and her muscles refused to obey.

He pulled her in a little deeper, and she let him, needing the heat pouring from him. His mouth, hot and hard, stole her breath, her balance…the sharp edge of her fear. Sensations, like something numb prickling back to life, battered her in a tantalizing torture as powerful as the pounding falls. Closed off behind the curtain of water, nothing felt real, except him.

She hadn't kissed a man, hadn't really missed that kind of intimacy, in over ten years. But here in the middle of nowhere, being kissed by a near-stranger, on the brink of possible death, her dormant libido was flaring to full, vibrant life. How insane was that?

She let her head fall limply to his shoulder while every cell of her body hummed for more. Her son was missing, in danger. Hunters intent on killing them were pursuing them. And all she could think of was Sabriel, touching her, kissing her, loving her.

The insanity of it bubbled up in rocky laughter. Sabriel's heartbeat, hard and strong against her chest, echoed the pulsing of life in her veins. She was alive. She wanted to stay alive. She wasn't beat. The Colonel might have her scared and hiding, but he hadn't broken her. She would keep going. She would find Scotty. She would save her son. And he would have the good life he deserved. They both would. Somehow.

"Sorry," she said. "I haven't kissed a man in a long, long time. I forgot what it was like."

"Pretty damn good."

Oh, yeah. "And this—" She stretched a hand tentatively toward the water. "This is just crazy. I don't usually go around kissing—"

"Don't make excuses."

There were none in his eyes, she noticed. Only the hot gleam of male hunger. An answering stab of female desire rocketed a shot of heat low in her belly.

"When this is over…" she said.

"We'll finish what we started."

She swallowed hard against the sensual shudder that fluttered from head to toe. "Okay."

It—her, him, them—wouldn't go anywhere. He was Tommy's friend. He'd see that this was just madness prodded by adrenaline. When they returned to civilization, he'd forget his promise. And she wouldn't remind him.

They stood there, arm in arm, until the fire's red light drained and the curtain of water shielding them darkened with night.

"Let's get out of here," he said. "They've lost our tracks or they would have found us by now."

Unable to talk, she nodded.

"Easy, now." His solid hands guided her. "Turn around, slowly."

She concentrated on her feet, lifting one, placing it solidly on the narrow shelf, then the other, not on the sheer wall of rock or the spume of water fermenting below. She pressed her back against the cold cliff, hands splayed out for balance.

"You've got it," he said, his voice a soothing murmur above the roar of the falls.

He had to let her go for that last turn of shoulder and hip. The loose pack shifted. The strap slipped on her shoulder. The unexpected drag lurched her to the side. Her boot skated against the slick rock. Her arm pitched out, jacking her upper body. Sabriel steadied her, but the pack's momentum ripped it off her back. "No! Scotty's medicine!"

Before she could think, before Sabriel could stop

her, she was airborne, plunging after the pack that was her only focus.

The cold slap of water shocked the breath out of her lungs. The foaming, frothing roil blinded her, rammed up her nose, filled her mouth. The force of the water-fall slammed her deeper and deeper, until she battered and skewered against the granite bottom. She swiveled her head from side to side.

The pack! Where's the pack? Scotty's medicine!

She pushed up, seeking light and air and the blue backpack. Something tugged at her foot, wouldn't let it go. She reached down, to find the heel of her boot jammed between two boulders. The shift and sway of the water spun and swiveled her body.

Her lungs burned. Her head exploded with white light.

SABRIEL DOVE IN after Nora, desperately searching for her in the opaque churn of water, fighting the current, the cold, the spin of images filling his brain. Anna, her limp hair, her slack body, her mouth open, foaming with bloody froth.

Anna, 503 feet down in the sea, pulling the pin to release the sled, opening the valve on the air tank to lift the bag that would take her up to the surface. But the bag didn't inflate. Oxygen dwindled. Her lungs expanded, exploded.

And he wasn't there to help her, he wasn't there. His vision blurred. His mind fogged.

He'd promised her he'd keep her safe. He'd promised her the Colonel couldn't get to her. He'd promised...

A flash of something dark, struggling against the water. *Not Anna. Nora. You're here. You're not too late.*

He swam. *Hang on, Nora.*

In her panic she was running out of air. Her wild gestures pointed down. Her foot was caught. He grasped her face in both hands, forced her to look at him, then willed her to stop fighting.

Eyes, big and wide, she grabbed on to his shoulders, and he could feel her begging for her life.

Trust me, Nora.

He dove. His heart pounded. Panic could kill her. He had to free her before the instinctual need for air had her gulping water. Fighting the unrelenting press of the water, its numbing cold, he slashed at her laces with his knife, released her foot, then shoved her toward the surface.

With a hard tug, he yanked her boot from its rocky hold and swam back up.

Gasping for air, he searched the river for Nora, found her sputtering and floundering, sliding with the current. Arms and legs sluggish, he crawled toward her, grabbed the collar of her fleece and tugged her to him.

Floating on his back, he searched the banks, let the current carry him to a bend, let it slam him against the mud. Fighting the muscle-numbing cold, he dragged Nora up the steep bank on the opposite side from the embers of a dying forest fire.

Sitting on the bank, gasping for air, he held her across his lap, one arm around her waist, the other pressing her head to his chest, and he kissed the top of her head. He thought he'd lost her.

Her kiss earlier under the falls, so sweet and so hungry, had threatened his well-being as much as the predators on their heels. He'd let it distract him, tumble his thoughts. And he'd almost lost her.

She looked ridiculously beautiful wet as a river rat. The sight of her breathing, alive, made his heart ache in a bittersweet way and that was wrong, all wrong for a man who choked on strings.

"My pack!" She fought his hold, aiming for the river.

He refused to let her go. "Forget the pack."

"I can't." Her teeth chattered like a runaway train. "Scotty's medicine."

He had to get her warm before hypothermia killed her. "We'll manage without it."

"*He* needs it."

"There are others ways to give him first aid if he needs it."

"No, it's not okay." Distress convulsed through the slur of her voice. "He could *die*."

"We need to get you warm or *you'll* die." He scanned the woods, searching for the Colonel's men. The bursts of their shouts blitzed through the air, but in this ravine sound carried and bounced, and he couldn't tell where or how far they were. "We have to get some cover or the Colonel's men will find us."

"Scotty…" Her mouth trembled. Her eyes were huge. Her lips were turning blue.

"I'll take care of him." Sabriel scooped her tight in

his arms with a desperation that he didn't want to think about. "I'll take care of you."

As the shivers trying to jump-start heat quaked through her body intensely enough to register on the Richter scale, a hole opened in his chest. He couldn't stand the thought of letting her down. The way he'd let Tommy down. The way he'd let Anna down.

RELIVING THE IMAGE of the pack floating away from her grasp again and again, Nora followed Sabriel blindly, weaving as if she'd had too much champagne. The lingering scent of smoke from the forest fire made the air hard to breathe. The steaming charred tree trunks forged a landscape straight out of a nightmare.

She hugged the crackling space blanket he'd dug out from his wet pack after she'd insisted she could walk on her own, but felt no warmth. Her fingers were stiff. Her legs filled with cement. Her frozen muscles ripped with each tetanic contraction against the cold.

Her purpose, her identity, her watch, her precious locket containing Scotty's picture—had all gone down with that pack. She gulped, trying to dislodge the lump in her throat. Scotty's medicine. Getting it to him had been the whole reason to come along. How did she expect to win a fight for Scotty's custody when she couldn't hold on to her son or to his medicine?

If she lost Scotty, it would be her own fault.

No, she told herself sternly, fighting the cold and the fatigue that cramped her muscles. She forced herself to take one more step. And another. Until her head throbbed as if her skull had shrunk around her brain and her throat bled from holding in her grief so that it wouldn't spill out, exposing her broken soul.

Sabriel stretched out a hand and helped her over a tangle of roots. "Can you walk a little longer? I want to get to those big boulders over there, so we can hide the fire from horizontal observation."

"I thought you said no fire."

"This is an emergency."

"Won't the Colonel's men see the smoke?"

"Chances are slim the way I'm going to rig it up."

Knowing a fire was imminent, the cold didn't bother her as much as it had only a few moments ago. *I'm going to be warm again. Soon, I'm going to be warm.* Warmth would help her function and functioning would get her back on the trail to Scotty.

She shuffled along, hunched over, head bent down, and it seemed to take endless minutes to reach their destination. Head still bent down, she ran into Sabriel's pack, looked up expectantly and saw the nice flat ground behind the ring of boulders.

"Is this where you tell me to take my clothes off and tell me body heat is the only way to get warm?" she asked through the knocking of her teeth.

"This is where I tell you to take off your wet clothes so the cold doesn't sap what little warmth you have left. I make you hot soup. Then I build a fire to dry your clothes."

He unfolded his sleeping bag from the dry bag in his pack and unzipped it so it made one big blanket. "Come on, get out of your clothes, then wrap up in this bag."

He turned his back to give her privacy, took out his small stove and got water boiling to make the soup.

"It's a cliché, you know," she said as he stirred a soup packet into a cup of hot water and she discarded the last of her wet clothing.

"What's a cliché?"

A shiver racked through her body and her clacking teeth added a background of castanets to her speech. "Falling into cold water, having to use body heat against hypothermia."

Amusement lit fire in the green of his eyes. "Have some soup."

"Books and movies." She sighed at the warmth of the soup against her frozen hands. "I've seen the situation a dozen times."

"Is that so?" He wrapped the space blanket over the top of the sleeping bag.

How crazy was it that she was disappointed he didn't lean over and kiss her as he had under the falls?

As shivers rattled her bones, her teeth, her brain, she sipped the burning soup. He gathered dry wood, started a fire, propped branches to form a lean-to. Heat radiated against the boulder behind her. But it wasn't enough. The cold went too deep.

She told herself it would have to be enough. She needed to survive.

Sabriel gathered his pack and slung it on his shoulders.

"Where are you going?" Nora asked.

"I'm going to make sure we hear anyone coming close."

The Colonel's men, he meant. When they didn't find their burned bodies, they would come looking for them.

Sabriel returned half an hour later, poured another cup of soup for her. He stepped out of his clothes, down to his boxer briefs, then draped them against the lean-to that held her. His long, lean limbs sparked a terrible and inappropriate yearning. For body heat, she told herself, but it was more than that.

Thoughts fizzled as he came closer, a warrior brave in all his glory against the backdrop of a rising moon.

She silently unclamped a corner of the crinkly blanket and sleeping bag, invited him in. He was cold, too, she rationalized. The sooner they both warmed up, the sooner they could go after Scotty.

Then she made the mistake of looking into Sabriel's eyes. They turned dark under the light of the moon, the bucking light of the fire, watchful, a hunter taking stock of a cornered prey. The wide-open pupils stirred with something dangerous, something barely controlled, and a spark of fear lanced her stomach as he settled beside her under the blanket, thigh-to-thigh, shoulder-to-shoulder, body hard and strong.

"It won't go further than this," he said, his voice strangely gruff.

"No, no, it won't." She brushed away the rattails of her still-wet hair, fed off the fire's rising heat, off the heat he generated.

"Unless you want it to."

Her pulse leaped. Her throat went dry. She was back under the water, the falls pushing her down, pounding her against the rocks, her breath gone, her mind a whirl.

A duel clashed—yes, no. You're crazy. Not the right time. Not the right place. Not the right man. Then, yes, please, yes.

She leaned into his shoulder, kissed the jumping pulse at the hollow of his neck. Pine and mint and musk had never smelled so good.

His hand skimmed her throat, his palm rough against the tender skin, and she turned, exposing more of her vulnerable neck. This crazy response had to stop. She was a mother. She had a child to save.

A body to warm.

His hands rubbed and stroked, spread a tingling sensation across her frozen limbs. Her breasts swelled, ached. Just life coming back. But, oh, it felt so good. She hadn't realized how long she'd been half-alive, how long she'd pretended that settling was enough. Closer, she needed him closer. She arched into him. Her gaze connected with the green fire of his.

"Please," she said. "Don't stop."

SABRIEL WANTED to do something, anything, to soothe away the fatigue and fear lining her face. He should stop. He should warm her another cup of soup and leave it at that. But it was more than soup he wanted to give her. The need ran through him in a fever, made him shiver. He had no right to feel this way. No right to want her. She was his responsibility. She was depending on him to save her son's life.

He shouldn't care or want or need.

But he did.

And the last thing he needed with Boggs so close was to get lost in the all-consuming dark pools of her eyes. Not while the part of his brain that was still operating was screaming that she was in danger.

Under the heavy white gaze of the moon, she stretched out beside him on the insulating bed of leaves he'd built for her. Her eyes, God, her eyes. Lost, gentle eyes. Their intensity, a pull he couldn't resist. And he forgot to close the gate, to shore up the fence. He forgot he didn't want to feel, couldn't afford to feel anything if he was to stay sane.

She anchored her hands to his neck, arched her body to his and opened like a flower to receive him. He sighed, gave in to his weakness.

Her smooth, soft skin slid under his palms. He made himself taste. He made himself touch. But all the savage edge cutting through him wanted was to devour. Hunger he hadn't known was that sharp, that ravenous bolted through him, stripping all common sense.

Her response spanned the scale from shy to eager until he was as twisted around as she was. The depths of those big, brown eyes sucked in his darkest emotions, fading them, and the part of him he'd fenced in after Anna's death broke loose.

He moved into her, and she moaned, giving herself to him, not a surrender, but a reel that took him higher and higher until he could finally breathe free.

THE HEAT OF THE FIRE, reflecting off the boulders behind them, the insulating thickness of the leaves, made their hideaway a snug nest that had Sabriel almost too hot.

Body loose and warm, Nora traced the fineline tattoo of a tiger on his left pelvic girdle, gave equal attention to the intricate dragon decorating the right side. He remembered the day he'd walked into the tattoo parlor and, with each prick of the needle, renewed his resolution to go on living. Each design had taken six painful hours under an artist's hand and turned his life in a new direction.

"What do they mean?" she asked him, her speech unslurred now that she was warm again.

"Strength, loyalty, dedication and fierceness in battle."

"From your Army days?"

"After. To remind me that life is a precious gift. That I had to keep fighting." That he could not let evil win.

"Mine isn't as fine as yours."

"Yours?" He arched a brow.

She rolled over until he could see the faded blooming lotus at the base of her spine. "I had it done at seventeen." She laughed a short, sharp laugh. "I wanted to look older, wiser."

He traced the twining vine with a finger, felt her shiver of desire electrify him all over again.

He'd been careful, so careful, not to let anyone too close, not to get sucked into a relationship that would strangle him. He liked doing what he liked when he liked, not having to check in with anyone whenever he wanted to head to Boston, or the mountains, or to any damn place he pleased. Marriage might work for Falconer or Reed or Skyralov, but it hadn't worked for him.

And he wasn't in love with her. His stomach roller-coastered in a painful flux of tenderness. He cared, sure, but that wasn't the same as love, and he shouldn't mistake one for the other. With her big, brown eyes and her kiss-me mouth and that surprising brace of steel in her spine, she'd already taken chunks out of his hide.

His tight control over his personal space had slipped because of the situation and the stress and the fact that body heat *was* the most efficient way to deal with hypothermia.

Survival required desperate measures.

He didn't need the responsibility of a woman in a heapful of trouble. And she didn't need a man without a heart. She needed time to heal, time to find her legs, time to realize she had more grit and gumption than the Colonel had led her to believe in all those years of relentless control. Sabriel couldn't give her what she needed.

He rubbed at the irritation cramping the back of his neck. He'd known she was trouble, hadn't he? From the second his phone rang. Breathing room. They both needed it. And she'd need a way to save face and pretend this hadn't happened. He slid out from under the sleeping bag blanket.

"Where are you going?" The bloom of good sex still painted her cheeks the pink of desire.

"Tending the fire," he said, and found his irritation going up a notch at his defensive tone. "Sleep while you can. We need to get moving soon."

He closed his eyes and reached for her, planting a soft

kiss on her forehead. Her skin was warm and soft and tasted just this side of heaven. His brain started to fog and his body to yield. Hell, he was sunk.

THOUGH HE'D MEANT to stay awake, his body and brain had rebelled and he'd fallen asleep next to Nora. He stirred awake to the sound of silence.

Nora's body was folded into his in the nest of leaves and sleeping bag and space blanket. His hand guarded her heart, his pulse beating in time to hers. Her hand covered his, keeping it in place.

A Ranger sleeps with one eye and one ear open. How fast he'd shed all of his training. Slowly he sat up and reached for the dry clothes on the lean-to.

No hush of whispering trees. No song of birds. No busy scamper of squirrel. Just the eerie quiet of doom.

The fire was down to embers. Night hadn't yet crowned with the pale light of dawn. The scent of storm weighed the air. And the hairs on the back of his neck writhed in warning.

Then the world cracked with the terrifying sound of a landslide.

Chapter Twelve

"Get up," Sabriel said, shaking Nora's shoulder. "We have to go."

"What's wrong?" She sat up groggily, frowning. "What's that noise?"

"Our alarm. The Colonel's men are back. They triggered one of the tripwires I rigged up." He threw her clothes at her, then smothered what remained of the fire with dirt. "We have to head back to the falls."

"Why?"

"That's where the next sign is."

There wasn't time to argue or discuss, so he didn't give her any. He grabbed the sleeping bag, stuffed it in the pack and hustled her toward the river into the fog of dawn. Knowing the toll Nora's fall into the water had taken on her body yesterday, he hated to push her, but he had no choice.

At the river, he "slipped the stream" to lay a false trail, then entered the river on rocks. Nora gamely keeping up with him, he moved upstream, staying in the center, to prevent floating debris and silt from compromising the direction of their travel, then walked out backward.

At Toby Falls, Tommy's sign pointed them to a rickety shack old Will used as his summer home base. Illegal on federal land, but Will wasn't one to care about most people or rules. And some official would have had to find it—and him—to hand out a fine. Something that wasn't too likely.

"We can go two ways," Sabriel said as he destroyed Tommy's sign. "We can go the short, hard way and save an hour, or go around an easier climb."

"Short is good."

Her skin was still pale and he didn't want to push her too hard. "You've got to speak up if the climb gets to be too much."

"I can keep up." *I have to,* her determined eyes said, and he had to admire her perseverance.

"All right. You lead. See that Y-shaped maple?"

She nodded.

"Head there, and we'll take a reading."

By the time they reached the overgrown Lancet Trail Will had forged decades ago, the wind had risen to a howl, making their forward progress difficult.

Nora's pale, drawn face worried him. He could feel the drive ebbing out of her. So he prodded, cajoled, egged until the spark of fight came back into her eyes.

At noon, they reached the abandoned shack. He'd half expected Tommy to be there waiting with Scotty, but the building was empty. And he didn't like the distressed tracks or the sign of a jag of lightning burned into a leaf he saw on the ground.

Sabriel swore, his tirade echoing like an enraged bear. Tommy putting himself in danger was one thing, but putting his son in harm's way was reprehensible.

"What's wrong?" Nora asked, voice trembling.

"Tommy's going to Lightning Point." The point on Mount Storm that held a record for the most lightning strikes.

"That's bad?"

"That's where the Colonel caught us."

Nora pressed the lightning jagged leaf against her heart. "Why would he go there?"

"Damned if I know." Tommy's track was too predictable. The Colonel would have men patrolling the area—just in case. What the hell was he thinking?

"Scotty?" The hollow of her throat bumped with the hard beat of her heart. "He's still okay?"

"He's still keeping up with Tommy."

Scotty's tracks had started dragging about a mile back and Tommy had slowed down to match the boy's pace. Scotty was getting tired. The excitement of his adventure had worn off. And the hitch of heel and deeper press of toes seemed to indicate his little lungs were working harder than they should. Something Sabriel didn't dare share with Nora. Her anguish would slow them down and tracking fast had suddenly become a matter of life and death.

The rising wind seemed to laugh as they climbed the trail.

Sabriel let Nora continue to lead, to catch her in case she fell on this treacherous footing. The switchbacks took them to a ridge that meandered across a plateau and pushed up to a short, steep pitch that landed them on the edge of cliffs straight out of a monster movie. Adding to the horror effect were the birches that looked as if they'd been hacked willy-nilly by an angry giant.

"What happened to the trees?" Nora asked, gawking up at the broken crowns.

"An ice storm raged through a couple of years back." Leaving behind the gray ghost of dying trees.

He didn't like being here while the wind keened and whistled through the trees. "Let's keep moving."

Nora bent down to pick up a length of red rope that ended in a complicated knot covering a bubble gum-sized marble. "This is Scotty's monkey fist." She fingered the dirty marble. "Tommy showed him how to make it. He carries it everywhere with him."

Scrutinizing the writhing of amputated limbs above, Sabriel tugged on her sleeve. "We have to get out of here."

But with a strangled cry, Nora ripped out of his grasp and fell to her knees. She clutched at something he couldn't see and gasped. Her wide brown eyes turned to him. "It's Scotty's inhaler."

Gulping, she shook the container and pressed on the top. Nothing came out. Her throat bobbed and her voice broke. "It's empty."

Overhead, a thread of sound like a hem ripping.

A dry-bone snap. Sabriel grabbed Nora's arm, shoved her out of the deadfall's way. The trunk of a birch smashed next to them, thundering against the granite. As the trunk rolled, a stray branch whipped out, cracked him on the side of the head and sent him flying. He fell hard on his side. The thin skin of earth gave way under him, carrying him down across the slippery surface of the boulder. He braced his feet to slow his descent. His hands sought purchase on knobs and knots, and found none.

With nothing to stop the pull of gravity, he went right over the edge of the cliff.

"SABRIEL!" Nora, flat on her stomach, every muscle trembling, crawled to the edge of the granite slab and peered carefully over the edge. Sabriel hung on an arm of rock jutting out from the sheer side of cliff with only the pitiful hemlock sapling to give him a handhold.

"I'm okay," he said

"You're bleeding." The blow or the fall had cut his cheek, blood painting him a warrior-stripe of red.

"Just a cut."

"Just a cut doesn't lose you a gallon of blood so fast."

"Head wounds always look worse than they are." He moved slowly and shook off the pack. From the inside, he unwound a rope. "I'm going to throw this rope up to you."

With an awkward sideways throw, he launched the rope up the cliff.

Grimly, Nora wrestled with the rope that came snaking up at her. "Are you hurt anywhere else?"

"I'm fine. I just need to rest for a bit." He attached the pack to his end of the rope. "Nora, listen to me carefully. You'll have to go to Mount Storm and catch up to Tommy before he gets there. Otherwise, the Colonel will get him."

"I can't leave you here." The way he hobbled awkwardly on his left foot as he threw the rope up, figuring out he'd hurt his ankle didn't take a genius. Was it broken? Would infection set in before she could come back with help?

"You don't have a choice unless you want to lose Scotty," he said.

She couldn't risk losing Scotty. The fast closing of her throat had her taking a too-big gulp of air. "I need you."

"You've been leading all day."

"Because you were there to correct my mistakes."

"You know the songline."

She shook her head, not bothering to wipe the tears as she furiously worked to free the pack so she could tie off the rope to a tree for leverage and pull him up. "I can't leave you like that."

"Give it to me, Nora. Give me the song."

"What if you go into shock? What if you fall off that ledge?" What if he died?

"Give me the song, Nora."

She kept knotting the rope around the sturdiest trunk she could find. "'Pinball Wizard,' 'Don't Stand So Close to Me.' 'Stones in the Road' lead to a 'Landslide.' 'All Things Must Pass' until you're 'High and Dry'…." She gave him his song, verse by silly verse. "'Divided Sky,' look 'Heaven's Right There.'"

"Look where you've been," Sabriel reminded her. "Make up a line, then focus on where you're going. For Scotty."

"I'm sending down a rope." She dribbled the rope so it wouldn't lash him on its way down.

"Honey, you don't have the upper-body strength and I don't want to have to go fish you off the side of this cliff, too."

For an instant, she was sixteen again, watching her mother drive away, her gut twisted in a knot, hoping the car would turn around, knowing that it wouldn't. And she could *not* do this to Sabriel. Could *not* turn her back and walk away when he needed help.

"Only you can reach Scotty in time." Sabriel's voice was gentle, too gentle, and it made the tears flow again. "That was the whole point of this exercise, wasn't it? Finding Scotty?"

Reality crashed down on her as if another ghost tree had fallen. He was right. She had no choice. He could survive where he was. As a Ranger he'd suffered through worse. Heck, he'd lived in these wilds for a whole summer, evaded the Colonel and his trained men for a whole summer. He'd lived through the Colonel's revenge.

Scotty couldn't defend himself, and she wasn't sure enough of Tommy's state of mind to take the risk that he could protect their son. She would come back once Scotty was safe, and she and Tommy could pull Sabriel up.

Her conscience chafed. *You're doing to him what you swore you'd never do to anyone.*

"You don't have much time left before the Colonel's men catch up." Though Sabriel tried to hide the urgency in his voice, it climbed up rope and vibrated against her palms, bringing the whole nightmare back in vivid three-dimensional color.

"You're a sitting duck where you are." Her voice cracked.

"There's enough scrub here to hide me."

A few dead hemlocks clinging to the cliff's side? He was trying to calm her down, to give her a reason to go. The truth was that if the Colonel's men caught up to either of them, she and Sabriel would be killed.

Torn in half, she dragged up the rope.

"I'll be right back," she said through the mist of her tears. "And I swear, if you die before I get back, I'll kill you."

He laughed. "That's my girl."

She'd put him in danger. And now she had to make it right. She had to find Tommy and Scotty. Fast. She had to bring them back to free Sabriel.

In the bear bag, she lowered the first-aid kit, most of the food, the stove with the barrel filled with water.

"Keep it," he said, pushing the bag back up. "You'll need it."

"I don't have time to haul it back up. Besides, I can't carry a pack that heavy."

"Nora, don't be a fool."

I already am. Because losing him would hurt. And she was still going to leave him wounded and bleeding. Scotty had to come first. She shouldered Sabriel's pack, swallowed hard and turned her back to the cliff.

"It's almost eight miles to Lightning Point," he said. "It should take you about seven hours to get there."

Seven hours on her own in woods that might as well be an alien planet. She gulped.

"I'll come back." She curled her hand tight around the pack's straps. "I promise."

"I'll be waiting."

The first step away from the cliff was the hardest. She wanted to cry. *Hold it back. Choke it down. Concentrate.*

The wind mocked her.

Please, please, give me the strength to help Sabriel and to help Scotty.

She focused on the songline and took another step and another, the angry whip of wind battering her as if to test her courage.

She'd never feared monsters under her bed, in her closet or knocking at her window. No, the monsters on the other side of her bedroom door were enough to keep her wide awake at night, building playlists the way other children might Lego. She'd survived then. She could do it now. For Scotty. For Sabriel.

The trail descended through spruce and hardwoods to a steep slope she had to cut with switchbacks— "Pinball Wizard." There, she found Tommy's next sign—"Don't Stand So Close to Me"—a wall of pebbles pointing her toward a narrow ravine, and she cheered her small progress. "One down."

Too many more to go.

Trees thrashed like mad harpies, prodded by the rant of the wind filled with chaos.

I'm scared, I'm scared, I'm scared. She jabbed the ground with her heels and kept heading down the gorge. "No, you're not!"

Yes, you are, but it doesn't matter. She was *not* going

to give up. Scotty and Sabriel depended on her. She couldn't let them down.

Stay safe, Scotty. Mommy's working hard to find you.

Stay safe, Sabriel. I'm not going to leave you there alone.

The narrow gorge climbed up steeply to a ridge. "Don't Stand So Close To Me." Then through woods that broke over a granite slab with broken views— "Stones in the Road." To a slippery slope that crumbled under her feet—"Landslide."

In the growl of wind, she thought she could hear the Colonel's voice berating her. *Look at you, you miserable piece of street scum. Tommy could have done so much better than you. You ruined him.*

Then Sabriel's, encouraging her. *Keep going. Follow the songline. That's my girl.*

The twin blasts of wind had her swinging from desperation to elation.

Focus. Focus on what you're doing right. Focus on where you're going. Focus on Scotty.

As she walked, she bolstered her confidence with all the reasons she had to be grateful—Scotty, Sabriel, water in her pack, dry clothes, healthy feet. "I will not fall apart. I will find Scotty and Tommy. I will warn them of the Colonel's men. And I will find Sabriel again. I *am* a survivor."

Maples, beeches and oaks gave way to red spruce and opened up to a granite ledge with lush caps of moss, lichen and lowbush blueberry, then ended abruptly in a cliff with views of valleys and mountains. Night fell.

Cliff faces, exposed slides, mountain capped with meta-morphic rock, made granite bald islands in a sea of forested peaks. The wind called like wolves, a howling, hungry beast.

She stopped to rest for a bit. How many miles had she gone? She'd lost her watch in the river and couldn't tell how long she'd been walking. The beauty of sky and stars choked emotions in her chest until a veil of clouds stole both.

She didn't want to be here, alone. Falling back on old habits, to go deep into her mind where she went at night when the ghosts crawled around her head, was tempting. Her teeth wanted to chatter. She wanted to curl up. She wanted to just let this nightmare pass.

And what? Let the Colonel win, let him get Scotty? Let Sabriel die after all he's done for you?

Out here, there was no one to help. All she had was herself. And if she failed, three others could die. With determination, she rose, grabbed a branch, fashioned a walking stick and put one foot in front of the other.

She remembered the pace Sabriel had kept, resting—rationing her strength just as she was her water.

Hunger took over, filling her with an intense need to stuff herself. She became intensely aware that all she carried with her was one of Sabriel's energy bars and a three-quarter empty bladder of water. She had to hang on to both as long as she could. "It's not like you're starving. You had lunch. And when you get back down the mountain, you can eat all you want. Anything you want."

To hell with dieting. To hell with all the Camden rules.

As hard as she tried to push away thoughts of food, her mind filled with the forbidden chocolate death dessert she'd indulge in when she got back. She was going to take a half-hour shower, blasting hot, then linger in peppermint bubbles for another. She was going to sheath herself in cashmere and silk and she was going to drink a gallon of hot tea in front of a roaring fire.

"Before or after the chocolate death?" she mocked herself, glad Sabriel couldn't see how close she was to falling apart.

Sabriel. There was another puzzle. What would she do about him? She'd come to depend on him too much, but the thought of letting him go opened a rip in her heart.

Her boots dislodged small stones that rattled like teeth. What was that noise? There it was again. Footsteps? The Colonel's men? No, nothing. Nothing but the wind and her imagination.

Hoohoohoo, hoohoo, hoo. An owl, just an owl.

"Nothing's going to hurt you out here. Sabriel promised all the animals were more scared of you than you are of them."

She reached the next point and played through Sabriel's song, looking ahead for the next clue and couldn't find the boulder shaped like a moose head minus one antler in the dark—not even with the moon's light coming in and out of the clouds. Had she taken a wrong turn? Misinterpreted a clue?

This wasn't happening to her. She wasn't lost in the White Mountains, searching for her son. She was at home safely in her bed. They both were. This was just another nightmare, and she'd wake up any minute now to the soothing green walls of her room.

Except that her aching feet, her screaming thighs and her sandy eyes made this nightmare much too real. She wanted to scream, swear, belt out all the forbidden vocabulary that had once seemed vulgar and now seemed appropriate.

She lashed her walking stick against a tree trunk and it broke. "Wow, now that was really effective, Nora. What next? Throw a tantrum? That's a waste of energy. Just keep going."

The next crest faced her with yet another endless tableau of mountains. Searching for breath, she rested both hands on top of her thighs.

She had no idea where she was, if she was heading in the right direction, if she'd ever find Scotty. She was both hot and cold. Her nose an icicle, her torso bathed in sweat. And under it all, a layer of numbness kept her from feeling anything at all. Decades from now some poor hiker would come across her bleached bones.

But what else could she do except keep going? She had to find Scotty. *One step at a time. Remember the song.* She had to get back to Sabriel.

She developed a pattern. *Twelve steps forward, look behind and look ahead, then forward one foot in front of the other.*

"One step at a time. Remember the song."

The slim saddle between the mountains carried the moans and whispers, as if a legion of ghosts shadowed her walk, waiting for her to stumble so they could feast.

Her gaze followed the line of clouds growing angrier as they tumbled closer.

Her eyes burned, her muscles cramped, her joints protested. Exhaustion—physical, mental, emotional—dragged her down. She would not cry. Never again. She was strong.

The moan of the wind, the simple rugged beauty of her surroundings, became her friends, her touchstones, that rhythm of nature unmarred by her chatting gave her strength to keep going.

She reached Tommy's next sign—a bird in flight, pointing her north—and looking out at the vastness of the mountains around her, something broke.

The air became charged with energy, coming off every tree, every rock, every atom of the sky. Like the hardening chocolate shell cracking on a scoop of vanilla ice cream until the melting confection oozed from the inside out.

Before her, all possibilities unfolded.

At that instant, peace flooded through her, and she knew with a deep certainty she would survive. She would find Scotty and Tommy. She would lead them back to Sabriel. And they would all get off this blasted mountain safely.

And she would never again let the Colonel dictate how she or Scotty should live their lives.

She would tell Sabriel that she cared for him, that once she got on her feet and settled somewhere with Scotty, she wanted a chance to see where their relationship could lead.

Coldly rational, she turned back to the woods, to the song that would lead her to Tommy and Scotty, then back to Sabriel. That would lead her to her true home.

She spotted the next sign—a flat table of rocks. Two more lines. She was almost there.

A crunch of leaves.

She spun around.

Pain split her skull.

Then darkness.

Chapter Thirteen

As soon as Nora left, Sabriel dug through the bear bag she'd dumped on him—the little fool—and found the small roll of duct tape he kept in the first-aid kit. Balancing himself carefully on the rocky shelf, he taped his sprained ankle and wrist.

Nora could do it. She could find Lightning Point. She'd learned fast and was motivated. But not knowing how fast the Colonel's men were moving tore him apart. Climbing off this cliff would be hell, but he didn't want to leave her alone any longer than he had to. Bad enough his mind ticked with the minutes flying by, messing with his concentration.

He found the first fingerhold and tested his bum wrist. Pain streaked up his forearm. Nothing he couldn't take for, what, seventeen, eighteen feet? He'd climbed higher, shinnying up the maple, trellis and drainpipe to the third-story window of his parents' brownstone as a teenager. The important thing was that he could get his wrist to hold his weight.

He tested the sprained ankle and blanked his mind, focusing on the cliff wall in front of him. The climb path opened up with clear handholds and toeholds. All he had to do was take them one at a time. Slow and easy.

But Nora, with her big, brown eyes and sweet mouth, intruded. The thought that Boggs was hunting her, that Boggs would deprive her of her child, that Boggs would kill her, hammered at him, weakened his grip. He had to reach her before the Colonel's men did. He'd promised to keep her safe.

Hang on, Nora.

He pulled himself up on the toehold and reached up for the next fingerhold.

Sending her out alone had ripped him to pieces, but he'd had no choice. He couldn't have her wait while he climbed out, not with the Colonel's men so close. And he couldn't risk her harming herself trying to help him. But if he lost her...

Don't think. Just climb.

As he hauled himself up another foot along the granite cliff, something shifted inside him. When had this happened? When had he started thinking that she'd be around after this was over?

Sure, he liked having her around, liked her questions, liked the way she caught on fast. And he liked the smell of her, the taste of her, the whole neurotic, tenacious package. And damn if he didn't like the way she looked at him with those big, brown eyes. Worse, he really liked the way she kissed him, fit around him, made him forget about fences. Adding a room or two on the cabin wouldn't take that much more work.

Panting, he stopped, hung on the rock like one of the blasted spiders he hated, forced himself to clear his mind. He couldn't let himself dwell on Nora, on his feelings for her, or he'd end up at the bottom of the ravine and useless.

One breath, two, and the dread dimmed enough for him to continue to climb. He would get to her in time. He would consider no other alternative.

Lost in the concentration of the climb, he didn't notice Boggs until his shadow dropped down to cover Sabriel's last fingerhold.

A worm of a smile twitched Boggs's mouth. Malevolence filled his eyes. He lit a cigarette, dragged on it until the end glowed red. "I figured something like this happened. No way a tough guy like you was going to let a woman find her own way in the big, bad woods." Boggs pointed the cigarette at him. "Chivalry, that's your weakness. Killed your wife. If you'd let her handle her own crap…" He lifted an eyebrow. "But you had to be the hero." He took another drag and puffed a cloud of smoke. "Killed your career."

"Thanks for the concern."

"Need a hand?"

"I'm good."

"I can see that." Boggs squatted and peered down. "I'm glad we're getting this chance to talk. I'd hate for you to die not knowing what happened to the girl."

Sabriel's jaw tensed.

"I've got two men shadowing her right now." Boggs

dripped ash on Sabriel's head. "Once she's shown us where the boy is, she'll have an unfortunate fall. Along with Tommy. Who knows when their bones will be found." The worm of a smile returned and he unholstered his pistol, looked at it fondly. "I was going to kill you, but then I thought, no. He has a right to know when it's all over."

Boggs squinted and scanned the horizon. "I do believe this is part of the flight path." His eyes sparked with wicked pleasure when they returned to pierce Sabriel's gaze. "When you hear a helicopter fly by, you'll know it's over. That you've lost everything all over again—Tommy, the girl." He stood up. "The boy."

Boggs dropped his cigarette on Sabriel's hand, then crushed it with the heel of his boot until bone ground into rock. "Can't risk a forest fire now, can we?"

Wincing against the searing pain, Sabriel fought for purchase. Boggs dug harder.

Pain pulsed in white-hot shards.

"Careful, now," Boggs said. "Don't miss the ledge. I'd hate for you to miss the show."

Sabriel lost his grip.

NORA MOANED and cracked her eyes open. Bald rock all around as barren as the moon. Was that snow over there? In October? Too early. What was she doing outside, anyway? She rolled over, anchoring the throbbing in her head with the heels of both hands against her temples. Her stomach revolted.

She pulled up on her hands and knees.

"Hold it right there."

In slow motion, she turned her head. The blurred muzzle of a pistol swam before her and she remembered the hit. She followed the length of black sleeve up to the hard face. Hutt. How long had she been out? The sky was dark with storm clouds, but it was still day. Not that it mattered. She was cornered. Her heart shook against the cage of her ribs. She was trapped with no hope of rescue.

She'd really messed up this time. Hutt was going to kill her, roll her body over the cliff and make her disappear. *Oh, Scotty.*

"Nora? Are you okay?"

"Tommy?"

Each movement hurt, but she focused on Tommy, hands tied behind his back, ankles shackled, his face black and blue as if he'd fought a mountain lion. Blood caked his blond hair and one eye was swollen shut.

"Scotty?" she asked and couldn't keep the panic out of her voice.

"He's okay. He's safe."

"Where?"

"Calm down. He's okay."

How did he expect her to calm down when he was tied up and she couldn't move without the whole earth tilting off its axis? With the Colonel's thug pointing a gun at them and Scotty missing? "He's alone. My, God, Tommy, how could you leave a ten-year-old boy alone in this wilderness?" *Just left him alone to wonder if you'd ever be back.* "He could die."

"He's safe." His face screwed up in pain. "I made sure."

She drew in a shaky breath. "Tommy, *please*. I have to know."

"Sabriel will find him."

Waves of anger and terror stormed through her. *Don't fall apart. Stay strong. There's only you now.* "Sabriel's hurt."

Tommy's curse was cut off by the throb of a helicopter, pulsing through the air in a rattling heartbeat. The black bird rose from the mountain's side like a raptor and settled its spindly legs on the gray granite. The wash of the rotors pummeled against her, kicked up silt into her eyes, lashed her hair about her face in a stinging whip. Two men, armed with rifles, as well as the Colonel, jumped out of its belly.

No, not him. Not now.

She wanted to speed through this nightmare, get to the end, get to Scotty. A fit of shakes rattled through her, beating her heart like a trapped bird. She was going to be sick. Right here. Right now.

A splash of cold wind tamped down the nausea.

Stay strong. For Scotty.

In this wind, she was surprised that the aircraft had been allowed to go up at all. But then the Colonel never played by the rules, and his pilot probably feared the Colonel more than the weather.

Hard reality was that her son was still missing, that she was on top of a mountain, surrounded by mountains, that she now had four weapons pointed at her skull. How the helicopter had gotten here didn't matter.

She wanted to live.

She wanted to find Scotty.

She wanted to see Sabriel again.

And if she wanted any of those things to happen, she'd have to be her own hero.

SABRIEL PULLED HIMSELF up and over the lip of the cliff, the press of wasted time flaying at him like a sharp knife in sadistic hands. Boggs's tracks were easy to find. Where was he heading? Why was he taking the long way to Lightning Point? Had Nora tracked the wrong line?

Ignoring the pain throbbing in his ankle, Sabriel moved parallel to Boggs's expected tracks, cutting in once in a while to check his progress. He reached the ridge soon after noon. In this exposed area, wind and cold whipped through the layers of his clothes, made him aware of every bruise, every broken finger. He'd lost the track and would have to cut again. Logic told him to go left, but something inside pulled him to the right. That inner voice had never failed him and, this late, he couldn't afford to second-guess or he'd risk disaster.

Just as he was about to give up and cut back to the left, a glint in the distance caught his eye. A gum wrapper. And right there, Boggs's track.

Fatigue, pain, worry played tricks on Sabriel's mind, skewed his thinking, made his movements reckless. The oppressive weight of time flickered the fuse of panic. He shook his head. *Stay sharp.* Giving in to the exhaustion was one step from sloppy and letting down his guard. One step closer to losing Nora.

He squatted next to a track, studying its unlikely path, when his spine stiffened in warning.

At the moment Boggs fired his weapon the track's truth blossomed into knowing. Sabriel had been running on pure emotions, and that had put him square in the path of danger. Boggs had been laying tracks, taking him away from Nora, circling in for the kill.

And for his mistake, Sabriel was going to die.

Reacting with pure instinct, driven by rage, he rolled to one side.

Instead of finding his chest, the bullet grazed his arm. A hot wire of pain unleashed the base animal in him, blinded sense and reason. Boggs plowed out of the trees seven yards away and came up for the kill, aiming his weapon right at Sabriel's face. Sabriel waited until Boggs's ego took him too close and swept his feet out from under him, disarmed him.

He hit Boggs with every ounce of power he had left. Fist connected with face. Punch after punch exploded out of him, until Boggs flopped like roadkill.

Sabriel tied him up to a tree so that any movement of cuffed hands and feet would rip off his balls.

Sabriel shook the fog of pain from his brain. He should've known what the track was telling him, that Boggs was on his tail, that Boggs had laid them down to suck him in and trap him. Beaten by a jerk that wasn't all that good a tracker. But he couldn't afford to let his emotions overshadow his thinking.

Sabriel cut tracks until he found Nora's and pushed himself to make headway until he was dead tracking—

following faster than she was moving. As the beating pulse of helicopter blades chopped at the air in the distance, he prayed he wasn't too late.

THOUGH THE COLONEL smiled, his expression did not light with friendliness. "Where's the boy?"

"I'll never let him go back to your asylum." Tommy turned to Nora. "That's what he wanted to do. He was going to drug you. Have one of his doctors testify that you were mentally unstable. Then once you were caged, Scotty would be his. I heard him, Nora." His gaze, the most sober Nora had seen it in years, implored understanding. "I had to get Scotty away from the mansion."

"You did the right thing, Tommy." *I just wished you'd trusted me with your plan.*

"Tell me where the boy is," the Colonel ordered.

Tommy struggled to his shackled feet and faced his father, steady eye to steady eye. "Never."

Tendons strained at the Colonel's neck. Icy anger darkened his voice. "You will obey a direct order!"

"You know what I learned in your house, Colonel?" Tommy asked, the fear that had cowered him all of his life gone. "I learned that I didn't matter. It took Nora to show me that I was worth loving. It took Scotty to show me what unconditional love was all about. It took leaving your choking rein to learn I was worth something."

"Then you learned nothing." A cold, hard smile crimped the Colonel's lips, then dissolved. He raised his rifle and pointed it at her. "Tell me where the boy is or I will kill her."

Tommy's head whipped in her direction. "Trust me, Nora."

"Last chance, Tommy boy." The Colonel took aim.

Tommy spit in his father's direction. "Never."

"Your choice." The Colonel squeezed the trigger.

Tommy lurched, launching himself at her.

She fell sideways. Her head ringing with the report of gunfire and the hard slap of granite. Her lungs emptied and she could not catch another breath. *I'm dead, I'm dead, I'm dead. Oh, Scotty, I'm so sorry!*

Tommy's heavy body smacked onto hers.

Warm blood stained the rock under her head.

SABRIEL CRAWLED to the edge of the scrub of jack pines, sliding silently on patches of lichen, being careful not to dislodge a stone that would attract the attention of the Colonel's men below.

Two men with rifles. Hutt with a pistol at Nora's head. Costlow threatening Tommy with his size and a branch big enough to knock out a bear. The Colonel with a pistol at his hip.

With all eyes on Tommy, Sabriel approached the sharpshooter standing on the helicopter's left, positioned to keep the Colonel in his sight, but out of view of his twin on the other side. Using one of the pressure points Grandpa Yamawashi had shown him, Sabriel took out the soldier and dragged him into the brush, leaving him so he could do no harm. Sabriel stalked to the right side of the helicopter, slipped under the nose, out of sight of the pilot, and stunned the second rifleman with a nerve pinch to the neck.

Two down, three to go. He slithered around the perimeter of the bare rock, positioning himself behind Costlow. Danger shot in the Colonel's eyes as he aimed his weapon at Nora.

Too far, Sabriel thought. *I'm too far.*

Tommy shoved Nora and took the bullet intended for her. Blood burst in an ugly red bloom on Tommy's chest before he collapsed onto Nora.

For a second Sabriel could do nothing more than stare.

The creep had killed his own son in cold blood. But Sabriel couldn't think about the blow now, couldn't let the sharpness of the pain detract him. Not with Nora the next target.

As Sabriel maneuvered in close to take out Costlow, Nora rose to her feet and his stomach dropped.

A furious aura of strength surrounded her. Yielding was dying, and she was not going to give another inch.

A still chill iced her voice. "You've just lost the one thing you wanted."

Then she moved.

Nora, no!

NORA SHOOK Tommy's limp body. "Tommy!"

Blood. So much blood.

"Nora… 'Gimme Shelter…' 'Norwegian Wood…' 'Atlantic City…'"

"No, Tommy, what have you done?"

She rolled him off of her, shed her fleece jacket and pressed it against Tommy's chest to stanch the flow. "Tommy! Talk to me."

"He's dead," the Colonel said, no expression tainting his voice. "And if you don't want to end up in the same condition, you're going to stand up, raise your hands and lace them on the back of your head. You will *not* cheat me out of my legacy."

Tommy's only chance of survival was for her to pretend he was dead.

The Colonel didn't care about Tommy. Didn't care about Scotty. Only about winning.

Her stomach curdled at the thought of Scotty growing up under the Colonel's thumb. Of her sweet boy cracking like Tommy. Or worse, hardening into a clone of the Colonel. There was no way she would simply hand her son over to him, hand him the power to shape her son into a monster.

She had to buy herself time. Tommy had saved her life. She couldn't waste his sacrifice. She had to find a way to save Scotty.

Soaked in fear sweat, she rose and did as the Colonel asked. "You've just lost the one thing you wanted."

"Scotty? No. I'll still find him." His eyes shone with triumph. Her flesh prickled. "As for Tommy, he's been lost for a long time. I simply put him out of his misery."

"I always thought soldiers had more control than the average person," she said, proud that her voice remained steady in spite of the fear trembling inside her. "But your impulsive act lost you Scotty. Only Tommy knows where Scotty's hidden."

"I have trackers who can find a needle in a haystack."

"Such brilliant trackers that they need three months to track down two inexperienced teenage boys."

He raised his rifle. "You're of no use to me."

"Yes, I am. I can find Scotty. Tommy gave me the song."

Her busy, busy mind spun, tumbled, reeled. The world shrunk to now, to the Colonel and his men, to the thwacking heartbeat of the helicopter blades. To this one moment in time where if she didn't rock the boat, she might as well die.

She'd gotten into this mess because of her past decisions. Choosing not to fight. Choosing to accept. Choosing to cause no ripple that would leave her alone in the dark.

This was not the role model she wanted for Scotty.

She took a deep breath. Another. Her damp hands wiped the side of her pants.

Darkness from the approaching storm brewed on the horizon. The wind belted a violent rap, tossing the helicopter off its perch like a toy, sending it hovering into the sky nearby.

"I'll give you Scotty and you'll leave me here. Alive."

To her ears, her voice sounded hard, convincing.

The Colonel's smile was ghastly. His laughter as sharp and sudden as ice cubes cracking in water. "I could kill you right here and nobody would ever find your corpse."

"You want your grandson to see you as a hero. You won't kill his mother within his eyesight. And you won't risk his spending a night alone out here. Not with this storm coming. Not when the cold could trigger an asthma attack and kill him."

"You think you can manipulate me?" the Colonel asked.

"No. You're too smart. You know that what I'm saying is true."

"Too little, too late, Nora." He approached, a hunter squaring off for the kill. "I gave you a home, shelter, prestige. I opened my home to you, even though you were nothing but street scum. I sheltered you, protected you, gave you all the advantages that come with the Camden name. All I asked in return was that you give me an heir."

"I gave you one. A beautiful, sweet boy."

"You were too soft on the boy. How is the boy supposed to grow a spine that way?"

His words glanced away against the new hard skin of her determination.

"You're right," she said. "I admit that I was weak. I should have stood up for Tommy when you threw him out and limited his visits with Scotty. I should have stood up for Scotty when you tried to push him beyond his abilities. I should have stood up for myself when you accused me of being a bad mother. I will always regret that weakness. No more. I won't let you ruin Scotty's life."

Logic collapsed, blanking her mind, disappearing into a vortex of pure instinct. Everything around her slowed, slowed, slowed, until her heartbeat drummed inside her head. Her hand reached into her pocket, wrapped around Scotty's monkey fist.

The Colonel's hand was steady on the grip. His finger curled around the trigger, tightened.

She launched Scotty's monkey fist with all of her strength and it found its target of the Colonel's eye.

The Colonel reeled back, recovered and pointed his gun once again at Nora's chest. Anger cresting in a powerful wave propelled her forward. With a warrior's cry, she jammed all the years of fear, hatred and fury into the Colonel's outstretched arm and rammed into her jailor's body as if it were nothing but a boneless uniform.

As they fell in a heap, the Colonel cushioned her landing. His elbow cracked against granite. His weapon fired wildly, three bullets strafing the air in a futile SOS. A fourth punctured the helicopter. The pilot's head smacked against the plastic bubble, splotching a web of red.

The helicopter dipped. The skid tilted, spun, unraveling a rescue ladder from the bird's belly. Then, like a jouster's lance, the skid aimed straight for Nora. She rolled off the Colonel to get out of the way.

Madness burning in his eyes, the Colonel lifted his weapon. Keeping tabs on the wayward helicopter, Nora kicked at the Colonel's wrist, forcing it into the path of the flaying ladder. The tangle of rope pulled tight around the Colonel's weapon and arm, diverted the gun's spew of bullets into the sky and hoisted him off the ground. He reached up reflexively with his free arm and grabbed a ladder rung. The pilotless bird pitched again, caught a swirling current of air, and spiraled out of control over the side of the mountain.

The Colonel's scream vanished in the explosion that boomed like thunder, shaking the whole valley.

Chapter Fourteen

Dead. The Colonel was dead.

He could take his own son's life and not blink.

He could ruin his grandson's life, and think he was doing him a favor.

Violent. Controlling. Tyrannical.

But he was dead. And she was free.

Nora rocked onto her shaky knees, her relief nothing more than a flicker as she expected the Colonel's men to take over where he'd left off. She frowned at the barren landscape. Where had all the Colonel's men gone? Scattered like the cowards they were now that their leader couldn't sign their paychecks? She snorted. That was so like them.

Then Tommy, lying there so still, met her gaze. She shot to her feet and ran to him. She dropped to her knees and moaned at the blood-soaked fleece and the heart-wrenching sound of air gurgling out of the open wound. Too much blood. Too much. "Tommy?"

"Nora," Tommy said, his voice no more than a thread.

"Stay still, Tommy. I'll get you help."

"Too late." He reached for her wrist. His grasp feeble and ice cold. "I did it…for you…. For Scotty."

"I know."

His eyes implored her. "I did good?"

"You were amazing."

"So were you. Nice shot."

Her throat jammed tight with tears. In this instant, he looked at peace—like the man she'd met and fallen in love with all those years ago. The man who'd made her think he was the answer to her fears, when all along she'd been his. She forgave him, forgave herself. They'd both been doing the best they could in a difficult situation. "The Colonel's dead. He can't hurt us anymore."

"Go find Scotty," Tommy said, his hand slipping from her wrist. "Tell him I love him."

"I'll tell him his father was a hero."

"Mission accomplished." With one last whoosh of air, Tommy went limp in Nora's arms. She checked for a pulse at his neck, but found none. Tears clouded her vision.

"Nora!" Sabriel's voice ripped through the air.

Too late, she noticed Hutt bearing down on her, gun raised.

SABRIEL TOOK the legs right out from under Costlow, knocked him out with a well-placed blow to the temple, binding him so he couldn't cause any more trouble, and was about to maneuver to Hutt when Nora launched Scotty's monkey fist at the Colonel.

Seeing Hutt take aim at Nora, Sabriel reached for his weapon.

Fear pressed on him like ice, dark and cold.

He was close, so close. He couldn't lose her.

Don't look at Nora. Concentrate on Hutt.

Sweating, cursing, pain jarring him with every step, with no time for finesse, Sabriel steadied his grip and aimed.

Hutt's pistol discharged with a boom.

NORA FLATTENED against Tommy's body. Hutt's gun went flying out of his hand. He fell, swearing and holding his hand.

From the rugged granite Sabriel arose, a wild man, streaked with dirt and blood, looking solid and competent. A beautiful, magnificent sight. He kicked Hutt's gun over the side of the mountain and tied him up.

She ran to Sabriel, held him with a ferocity that shook her to the core. Her breath sawed in and out of her lungs. "Are you okay?"

He nodded. "You?"

She kissed his brow, his eyes, his mouth until the legs went weak and her knees gave out and let him hold her tight until her jumbled thoughts wound back to sanity. She pulled away, hands clamped around Sabriel's biceps. "Tommy. The Colonel shot him. I think he's—" she gulped "—dead. Scotty. We have to find Scotty."

Sabriel gave her shoulders a bolstering squeeze. "Take it easy. We'll find Scotty." He released her, bent to check on Tommy, and cursed softly.

Grief whispered through Nora's voice. "He left a songline. 'Gimme Shelter,' 'Norwegian Wood,' 'Atlantic City.' Do you know what that means?"

"I know where it is." He covered Tommy with the crinkly space blanket, pressed his palm against the wound beneath. "I'll find your son, buddy."

She hugged her elbows, cold now that the heat of battle was gone. Tears rolled down her cheeks. "We can't leave Tommy here. Not like this."

"We'll get Tommy down," Sabriel promised as he rose and took her hand, infusing her with strength. "We'll get him home. After we find Scotty."

"Which way?" She looked around, scenery nothing but a blur. "Scotty's got to be scared, all alone."

Sabriel limped toward the pines. "It's not far. A cave hidden by some spruce trees with a view of the boardwalk around the Lake Atlas resort."

As they hurried as fast as they could down the rocky slope, the first drops of rain fell from the sky.

THE STORM RAGED, following them into the narrow col and into the spruce woods, across a brook to a granite loaf, then sputtered out as they reached a level area.

A beam of fragile light broke through the clouds, revealing the curled up shape of her son with his bright yellow jacket at the mouth of a cave, struggling to breathe. Nora flew to him, fell on her knees and scooped him in her arms.

"It's okay, baby, it's okay." She buried her face in his

hair, her chest hurting at the sight of his labored breathing. "Breathe, Scotty, breathe for Mommy."

But he wasn't okay, and he couldn't breathe. His tiny chest strained to reach for the next breath. His voice was a thin, gurgly wheeze. "Mom-my…"

Tears clouded her vision. Her fault. She'd lost his medicine. Now they were hours away from help.

Sabriel, using Boggs's satellite phone, called in coordinates, then unclamped her arms from around her son. "Let me."

"He needs medicine." Her throat burned. "He can't catch his breath."

Remembering the inhaler she'd found on the trail, she groped around her jacket pocket. There might be a drop, enough to help loosen the iron grip of inflammation in his lungs. "Sweetie? Look at me. I'm going to help you with your inhaler."

But all he could manage was another soul-wrenching wheeze. The pitiful sound was a knife to her heart.

"You're going to have to calm down, Nora, or you're going to make him worse."

A moaning wail tore from her as Sabriel gently extricated her son from her arms. "No."

"I can help him."

Magic hands, she remembered. They'd helped her. Maybe they could help Scotty. "What can I do?"

"Get the Jetboil and boil some water for coffee. It's a bronchodilator. It'll help open up his lungs."

She knew that. How could she have forgotten? She

rushed to pull the coffee grounds and the stove from the pack.

"Hey, Scotty," Sabriel said, his voice calm and gentle as he crouched next to her anxious son. "You don't know me, but I'm a friend of your mom's."

"Green-eyed man," Scotty wheezed. "Dad…"

"Shh. Don't talk. I'm going to try and make you breathe again, okay? I'm going to press on your back with my fingers, then on your chest. It's not going to hurt, just feel like you've got a marble stuck under your shirt."

Acupressure. *Please, please let it work.* Was it the force of her will or the figment of her imagination? Before the water had even started to boil, she could swear Scotty's breathing was less labored.

Sabriel moved his hands to cover his chest. "And it might feel hot or tingly."

Tears of relief overtook her anxiety as Scotty visibly relaxed and color returned to his skin.

"How's that coffee coming along?"

She poured the brew with shaky hands and handed it to Sabriel. "It's hot. Be careful."

Scotty drank and the wheezing lessened. She wanted to cheer at the miracle Sabriel had performed.

Dizzy with relief, she pulled Scotty into her arms and rocked him. *I found you, Scotty. I found you.*

Then she looked up at Sabriel and her heart squeezed hard. *I found you, too.*

Tommy was dead and because of him, she and Scotty were alive. The Colonel and his unyielding control were gone. And for the first time in…forever…she was at the helm of her fate.

In the distance the whir of helicopter blades sliced through the air. With a gasp, she searched the sky, ready to pull Scotty deeper into the cover of the cave.

"It's okay." Sabriel stood and sent up a flare to signal the pilot. "It's the cavalry. We need to get back to the clearing."

He reached a hand toward her. "Ready to go home?"

Her gaze filled with Scotty in her arms, breathing freely, and Sabriel at her side, solid and supporting— her fair-haired boy and her dark-haired hero—and her heart was at peace. "I'm already there."

Three weeks later.

THE BROKEN HAND was healing, but not fast enough for Sabriel's taste. Sitting, doing nothing wasn't his style. The immobilized finger joints made it impossible to work out his frustration pounding nails or sawing wood.

He wanted to see Nora. Be with her. But she needed time to find her own footing. Her and Scotty. Get used to their freedom. He wasn't good at strings anyway, he reminded himself, and she came with a whole ballful.

At the sound of a car bumping its way slowly down his dirt drive, Sabriel walked to the door and leaned against the door frame.

Stupid to feel nervous. It wasn't her. A navy SUV— one of Seekers' vehicles. Just Liv. Falconer's wife had made it her mission to provide him with casserole dinners so he wouldn't starve while his hand was healing.

A smile twitched at the corner of his mouth until the car door opened and long legs came out. His breath hitched. Nora. Coming toward him with a curious mixture of anxiety and anticipation. She looked good. More than good. Life painted her cheeks pink, shone gold in her dark hair, gleamed stars in her brown eyes.

Their gazes met. His stomach jittered. He tried to meet her halfway, but he couldn't make his legs move.

"How's Scotty doing?" he asked when she reached the walkway.

She stopped at the dirt path leading to the door, rocked on her toes, then back on her heels. "He's doing great. He hasn't had an asthma attack since we've been back. He's in a new school, making new friends. He even has a play date for the next hour or so. It's all good." A small smile curved her lips. "He's been asking for the green-eyed man Tommy told him he was sending to take care of him and me."

Tommy, Sabriel had found out through Kingsley's digging into Tommy's medical records, had been dying of a fast-moving cancer. He'd meant for Sabriel to follow him to the mountains, for Sabriel to find the signs to Scotty while Tommy faced the Colonel. Whether he'd planned to kill the Colonel or have the Colonel kill him, Sabriel would never know. The ultimate result, though, was meant to have been Scotty and Nora's freedom.

"I hear you got a job," Sabriel said, the words not quite what he had in mind.

Her smile widened and her eyes flared into a brilliant kaleidoscope of gold and brown. "Your friend Kingsley mentioned a job opening at a radio station in Keene. I'm working behind the scenes for now, but it's close to Scotty's new school and the hours are good."

"Sounds perfect."

"It is." The rocking increased, as if she wasn't sure if she wanted to move forward or go back. "I, uh, wanted to thank you. In person. For rescuing Scotty. For the loan of your apartment in Keene until I can get on my feet." She shrugged and shook her head. "For…everything."

"No problem." Big problem, actually. A thank-you note wasn't what he was looking for.

Her fingers knitted in front of her. She closed her eyes and huffed out a breath before turning those big, brown eyes at him. "It's fast, I know. Too fast. I don't understand it, really. But…" She licked her dry lips. "I want you, Sabriel. I love you. I'd like to…I'd like to see where you and me, well, where it leads."

Emotion clogged his throat and before he quite realized what he was doing, he'd taken the two steps separating them and gathered her in his arms. The sweet almond scent of her messed with his mind, the soft feel of her was a lightning rod straight to his gut, the potent taste of her blew down whatever fence was left around his heart. The thought of a future with a whole net of strings didn't seem scary. It seemed…like what he'd been waiting for. "God, I missed you."

"Is that a yes?"

"Hell, yes." He kissed hard and long, reveled in the

melting of her body to his, then slung an arm around her shoulder and turned her around. "What do you think about the house?"

She curled back into the circle of his arms. "It's beautiful."

"It's a work in progress." Like him. Like her. Like their future with Scotty and maybe another kid or two. "I've been thinking that maybe it needs an addition."

"Oh, yeah?"

"Want to see the inside?"

Her smile turned wicked. "I want to see it all."

He took her hand and led her over the threshold, her laughter tripping into the room the sweetest music he'd ever heard. A spoke of sun spilled through the skylight lighting their way. The empty hole inside him since Anna had died and the Colonel had tried to destroy his life filled with comforting warmth. Having Nora here in this house felt…right and good.

* * * * *

SABRIEL'S ENERGY BARS

1 cup rolled oats
1 cup of your favorite crunchy cereal
1/4 cup sesame seeds
1 1/2 cups chopped dried apricots
1 cup raisins
1/4 cup chopped almonds
1/4 cup wheat germ (or ground flaxseed)
1/2 cup protein powder
1 tbsp butter
3/4 cup brown rice syrup
1/2 cup almond butter
1 tsp cinnamon (or vanilla powder)

Preheat the oven to 350°F. Lightly spray a 9-x-13-inch pan with nonstick cooking spray.

Spread the oats, cereal and sesame seeds out on an ungreased cookie sheet and toast for about 10 minutes. Cool slightly, then transfer to a large mixing bowl. Add the apricots, raisins, almonds, wheat germ, and protein powder. Mix well.

In a saucepan over medium heat, melt the butter. Add the brown rice syrup, stirring until bubbly. Mix in the almond butter and cinnamon. Pour into the dry ingredients and quickly mix together and transfer to the prepared pan. Press the mixture into the pan and refrigerate for at least 4 hours. Cut into 12 bars and wrap each one separately in wax paper; store in the refrigerator.

* * * * *

**Every Life Has More
Than One Chapter**

Award-winning author Stevi Mittman delivers
another hysterical mystery, featuring Teddi Bayer,
an irrepressible heroine, and her to-die-for hero,
Detective Drew Scoones. After all, life on Long
Island can be murder!

*Turn the page for a sneak peek
at the warm and funny fourth book,
WHOSE NUMBER IS UP, ANYWAY?,
in the Teddi Bayer series,
by STEVI MITTMAN.
On sale August 7*

"Before redecorating a room, I always advise my
clients to empty it of everything but one chair.
Then I suggest they move that chair from place to
place, sitting in it, until the placement feels right.
Trust your instincts when deciding on furniture
placement. Your room should 'feel right.'"

—TipsFromTeddi.com

Gut feelings. You know, that gnawing in the pit of
your stomach that warns you that you are about to do
the absolute stupidest thing you could do? Something
that will ruin life as you know it?

I've got one now, standing at the butcher counter in
King Kullen, the grocery store in the same strip mall as
L.I. Lanes, the bowling alley-cum-billiard parlor I'm in
the process of redecorating for its "Grand Opening."

I realize being in the wrong supermarket probably
doesn't sound exactly dire to you, but you aren't the one
buying your father a brisket at a store your mother will
somehow know isn't Waldbaum's.

And then, June Bayer isn't your mother.

The woman behind the counter has agreed to go into the freezer to find a brisket for me, since there aren't any in the case. There are packages of pork tenderloin, piles of spare ribs and rolls of sausage, but no briskets.

Warning Number Two, right? I should be so out of here.

But no, I'm still in the same spot when she comes back out, brisketless, her face ashen. She opens her mouth as if she is going to scream, but only a gurgle comes out.

And then she pinballs out from behind the counter, knocking bottles of Peter Luger Steak Sauce to the floor on her way, now hitting the tower of cans at the end of the prepared foods aisle and sending them sprawling, now making her way down the aisle, careening from side to side as she goes.

Finally, from a distance, I hear her shout, "He's deeeeeeaaaad! Joey's deeeeeaaaad."

My first thought is, *You should always trust your gut.*

My second thought is that now, somehow, my mother will know I was in King Kullen. For weeks I will have to hear "What did you expect?" as though whenever you go to King Kullen someone turns up dead. And if the detective investigating the case turns out to be Detective Drew Scoones…well, I'll never hear the end of that from her, either.

She still suspects I murdered the guy who was found dead on my doorstep last Halloween just to get Drew back into my life.

Several people head for the butcher's freezer and I position myself to block them. If there's one thing I've learned from finding people dead—and the guy on my doorstep wasn't the first one—it's that the police get very testy when you mess with their murder scenes.

"You can't go in there until the police get here," I say, stationing myself at the end of the butcher's counter and in front of the Employees Only door, acting as if I'm some sort of authority. "You'll contaminate the evidence if it turns out to be murder."

Shouts and chaos. You'd think I'd know better than to throw the word *murder* around. Cell phones are flipping open and tongues are wagging.

I amend my statement quickly. "Which, of course, it probably isn't. Murder, I mean. People die all the time, and it's not always in hospitals or their own beds, or…" I babble when I'm nervous, and the idea of someone dead on the other side of the freezer door makes me very nervous.

So does the idea of seeing Drew Scoones again. Drew and I have this on-again, off-again sort of thing…that I kind of turned off.

Who knew he'd take it so personally when he tried to get serious and I responded by saying we could talk about *us* tomorrow—and then caught a plane to my parents' condo in Boca the next day? In July. In the middle of a job.

For some crazy reason, he took that to mean that I was avoiding him and the subject of *us*.

That was three months ago. I haven't seen him since.

The manager, who identifies himself and points to his nameplate in case I don't believe him, says he has to go into *his cooler.* "Maybe Joey's not dead," he says. "Maybe he can be saved, and you're letting him die in there. Did you ever think of that?"

In fact, I hadn't. But I had thought that the murderer might try to go back in to make sure his tracks were covered, so I say that I will go in and check.

Which means that the manager and I couple up and go in together while everyone pushes against the doorway to peer in, erasing any chance of finding clean prints on that Employees Only door.

I expect to find carcasses of dead animals hanging from hooks, and maybe Joey hanging from one, too. I think it's going to be very creepy and I steel myself, only to find a rather benign series of shelves with large slabs of meat laid out carefully on them, along with boxes and boxes marked simply Chicken.

Nothing scary here, unless you count the body of a middle-aged man with graying hair sprawled faceup on the floor. His eyes are wide open and unblinking. His shirt is stiff. His pants are stiff. His body is stiff. And his expression, you should forgive the pun—is frozen. Bill-the-manager crosses himself and stands mute while I pronounce the guy dead in a sort of *happy now?* tone.

"We should not be in here," I say, and he nods his head emphatically and helps me push people out of the doorway just in time to hear the police sirens and see the cop cars pull up outside the big store windows.

Bobbie Lyons, my partner in Teddi Bayer Interior

Designs (and also my neighbor, my best friend and my private fashion police) and Mark, our carpenter (and my dogsitter, confidant and ego booster), rush in from next door. They beat the cops by a half step and shout out my name. People point in my direction.

After all the publicity that followed the unfortunate incident during which I shot my ex-husband, Rio Gallo, and then the subsequent murder of my first client—which I solved, I might add—it seems like the whole world, or at least all of Long Island, knows who I am.

Mark asks if I'm all right. (Did I remember to mention that the man is drop-dead-gorgeous-but-a-decade-too-young-for-me-yet-too-old-for-my-daughter-thank-god?) I don't get a chance to answer him because the police are quickly closing in on the store manager and me.

"The woman—" I begin telling the police. Then I have to pause for the manager to fill in her name, which he does: *Fran.*

I continue. "Right. Fran. Fran went into the freezer to get a brisket. A moment later she came out and screamed that Joey was dead. So I'd say she was the one who discovered the body."

"And you are…" the cop asks me. It comes out a bit like who do I *think* I am, rather than who am I really.

"An innocent bystander," Bobbie, hair perfect, makeup just right, says, carefully placing her body between the cop and me.

"And she was just leaving," Mark adds. They each take one of my arms.

Fran comes into the inner circle surrounding the

cops. In case it isn't obvious from the hairnet and blood-stained white apron with Fran embroidered on it, I explain that she was the butcher who was going for the brisket. Mark and Bobbie take that as a signal that I've done my job and they can now get me out of there. They twist around, with me in the middle, as if we're a Rockettes line, until we are facing away from the butcher counter. They've managed to propel me a few steps toward the exit when disaster—in the form of a Mazda RX7 pulling up at the loading curb—strikes.

Mark's grip on my arm tightens like a vise. "Too late," he says.

Bobbie's expletive is unprintable. "Maybe there's a back door," she suggests, but Mark is right. It's too late.

I've laid my eyes on Detective Scoones. And while my gut is trying to warn me that my heart shouldn't go there, regions farther south are melting at just the sight of him.

"Walk," Bobbie orders me.

And I try to. Really.

Walk, I tell my feet. *Just put one foot in front of the other.*

I can do this because I know, in my heart of hearts, that if Drew Scoones was still interested in me, he'd have gotten in touch with me after I returned from Boca. And he didn't.

Since he's a detective, Drew doesn't have to wear one of those dark blue Nassau County Police uniforms. Instead, he's got on jeans, a tight-fitting T-shirt and a tweedy sports jacket. If you think that sounds good, you should see him. Chiseled features, cleft chin, brown hair that's naturally a little sandy in the front, a smile that…well, that doesn't matter. He isn't smiling now.

He walks up to me, tucks his sunglasses into his breast pocket and looks me over from head to toe.

"Well, if it isn't Miss Cut and Run," he says. "Aren't you supposed to be somewhere in Florida or something?" He looks at Mark accusingly, as if he was covering for me when he told Drew I was gone.

"Detective Scoones?" one of the uniforms says. "The stiff's in the cooler and the woman who found him is over there." He jerks his head in Fran's direction.

Drew continues to stare at me.

You know how when you were young, your mother always told you to wear clean underwear in case you were in an accident? And how, a little farther on, she told you not to go out in hair rollers because you never knew who you might see—or who might see you? And how now your best friend says she wouldn't be caught dead without makeup and suggests you shouldn't, either?

Okay, today, *finally,* in my overalls and Converse sneakers, I get it.

I brush my hair out of my eyes. "Well, I'm back," I say. As if he hasn't known my exact whereabouts. The man is a detective, for heaven's sake. "Been back awhile."

Bobbie has watched the exchange and apparently decided she's given Drew all the time he deserves. "And we've got work to do, so…" she says, grabbing my arm and giving Drew a little two-fingered wave goodbye.

As I back up a foot or two, the store manager sees his chance and places himself in front of Drew, trying to get his attention. Maybe what makes Drew such a good detective is his ability to focus.

Only what he's focusing on is me.

"Phone broken? Carrier pigeon died?" he asks me, taking in Fran, the manager, the meat counter and that Employees Only door, all without taking his eyes off me.

Mark tries to break the spell. "We've got work to do there, you've got work to do here, Scoones," Mark says to him, gesturing toward next door. "So it's back to the alley for us."

Drew's lip twitches. "You working the alley now?" he says.

"If you'd like to follow me," Bill-the-manager, clearly exasperated, says to Drew—who doesn't respond. It's as if waiting for my answer is all he has to do.

So, fine. "You knew I was back," I say.

The man has known my whereabouts every hour of the day for as long as I've known him. And my mother's not the only one who won't buy that he "just happened" to answer this particular call. In fact, I'm willing to bet my children's lunch money that he's taken every call within ten miles of my home since the day I got back.

And now he's gotten lucky.

"*You* could have called *me*," I say.

"You're the one who said *tomorrow* for our talk and then flew the coop, chickie," he says. "I figured the ball was in your court."

"Detective?" the uniform says. "There's something you ought to see in here."

Drew gives me a look that amounts to *in or out?*

He could be talking about the investigation, or about our relationship.

Bobbie tries to steer me away. Mark's fists are balled. Drew waits me out, knowing I won't be able to resist what might be a murder investigation.

Finally he turns and heads for the cooler.

And, like a puppy dog, I follow.

Bobbie grabs the back of my shirt and pulls me to a halt.

"I'm just going to show him something," I say, yanking away.

"Yeah," Bobbie says, pointedly looking at the buttons on my blouse. The two at breast level have popped. "That's what I'm afraid of."

REQUEST YOUR FREE BOOKS!

2 FREE NOVELS
PLUS 2
FREE GIFTS!

HARLEQUIN®

INTRIGUE®

Breathtaking Romantic Suspense

YES! Please send me 2 FREE Harlequin Intrigue® novels and my 2 FREE gifts. After receiving them, if I don't wish to receive any more books, I can return the shipping statement marked "cancel." If I don't cancel, I will receive 6 brand-new novels every month and be billed just $4.24 per book in the U.S., or $4.99 per book in Canada, plus 25¢ shipping and handling per book and applicable taxes, if any*. That's a savings of close to 15% off the cover price! I understand that accepting the 2 free books and gifts places me under no obligation to buy anything. I can always return a shipment and cancel at any time. Even if I never buy another book from Harlequin, the two free books and gifts are mine to keep forever.

182 HDN EEZ7   382 HDN EEZK

Name	(PLEASE PRINT)	
Address		Apt. #
City	State/Prov.	Zip/Postal Code

Signature (if under 18, a parent or guardian must sign)

Mail to the **Harlequin Reader Service®**:
IN U.S.A.: P.O. Box 1867, Buffalo, NY 14240-1867
IN CANADA: P.O. Box 609, Fort Erie, Ontario L2A 5X3

Not valid to current Harlequin Intrigue subscribers.

Want to try two free books from another line?
Call 1-800-873-8635 or visit www.morefreebooks.com.

* Terms and prices subject to change without notice. NY residents add applicable sales tax. Canadian residents will be charged applicable provincial taxes and GST. This offer is limited to one order per household. All orders subject to approval. Credit or debit balances in a customer's account(s) may be offset by any other outstanding balance owed by or to the customer. Please allow 4 to 6 weeks for delivery.

Your Privacy: Harlequin is committed to protecting your privacy. Our Privacy Policy is available online at www.eHarlequin.com or upon request from the Reader Service. From time to time we make our lists of customers available to reputable firms who may have a product or service of interest to you. If you would prefer we not share your name and address, please check here. ☐

HI07

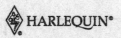

INTRIGUE®

COMING NEXT MONTH

#1005 CLASSIFIED BABY by Jessica Andersen
Bodyguards Unlimited, Denver, CO (Book 6 of 6)
It's all been leading to this! Nicole Benedict picks the worst day to tell Ethan Moore she's pregnant. Trapped together in PPS headquarters, they're seconds away from the building blowing up—along with PPS's largest investigation ever.

#1006 ANYTHING FOR HIS SON by Rita Herron
Lights Out (Book 3 of 4)
In the chaos of a citywide blackout, an act of revenge takes Ethan Matalon's son from him, and he will risk everything to get him back.

#1007 STANDING GUARD by Dana Marton
Mission: Redemption
When the government offers Samantha Hanley a clean record, she's partnered with tough-as-nails bodyguard Reese Moretti to take down the FBI's most wanted.

#1008 STORK ALERT by Delores Fossen
Five-Alarm Babies
Kelly Manning is stunned to learn that her infant might have been switched at birth with another. To get the truth means getting at single father Nick Lattimer, a Renaissance cowboy deep in a family struggle over a lavish Texas ranch.

#1009 UP AGAINST THE WALL by Julie Miller
The Precinct: Vice Squad
Vice Detective Seth Cartwright works undercover at the Riverboat Casino—an organized crime front that reporter Rebecca Page just might blow the lid off. Between these two, it's hard to tell where the strong wills end and the passion begins.

#1010 TAKEN by Lori L. Harris
After Jillian Sorensen and her sister stop to help an injured woman, they become the latest victims of white slavery. When only Jillian escapes, she must go back with attorney Rick Brady to rescue her sister and find out where all the missing girls go.